*Other Virago Modern Classics
published by The Dial Press*

Frost in May	Antonia White
The Lost Traveller	Antonia White
The Sugar House	Antonia White
Beyond the Glass	Antonia White
The Unlit Lamp	Radclyffe Hall
The Judge	Rebecca West
Harriet Hume	Rebecca West
The Lacquer Lady	F. Tennyson Jesse
The Beth Book	Sarah Grand
The Vet's Daughter	Barbara Comyns
The Getting of Wisdom	Henry Handel Richardson
Precious Bane	Mary Webb
The Semi-Attached Couple & *The Semi-Detached House*	Emily Eden

REBECCA WEST

THE RETURN OF
THE SOLDIER

New Introduction by
Victoria Glendinning

The Dial Press
New York

To
J

Published by
The Dial Press
1 Dag Hammarskjold Plaza
New York, New York 10017

Original edition copyright 1918 by Rebecca West
Revised edition © 1980 by Rebecca West
Introduction copyright © 1980 by Victoria Glendinning
All rights reserved.
Manufactured in the United States of America
First Printing

Library of Congress Cataloging in Publication Data

West, Rebecca, pseud., 1892–
The return of the soldier.

(Virago modern classics)
I. Title. II. Series: Virago modern classic.
PR6045.E8R4   1982   823'.912   81-15240
ISBN 0-385-27226-X   AACR2

INTRODUCTION

Rebecca West was 24 in 1918, when *The Return of the Soldier* was published. She was already well established as a journalist, and this was her second book; her first was *Henry James*, a short but assured and lively study that had come out two years before.

The Return of the Soldier too is a short book; on a first reading it is a simple and bitter-sweet tale turning on the loss of memory of Chris Baldry, the central male character, which makes him forget his charming wife and their ten years of marriage and remember only an earlier, humbler love. Loss of memory is a fictional device that is frequently abused in stories and films to facilitate mediocre plotting. It is important to remember that it was a frequent and frightening symptom of what is technically called "hysterical fugue", the "shell-shock" suffered by some soldiers as a result of the horrors of the trenches in the First World War. Rebecca West was writing her novel during that war; there was nothing fanciful or expedient in her use of such trauma.

Chris's fugue, or flight, was not only from the grim realities of war; it was from the apparently pleasant reality of his marriage. It seems to me that he himself, seen in the novel only through the uncritical eyes of love, is not an interesting character; he is the epitome of English masculine fineness, virtue and charm, a love-object. The interest and the tension of the book lie in the three women who, in their crucially different ways, care about him.

The background of Baldry Court, where Kitty his wife and Jenny his cousin—the narrator—wait for Chris's return, is built up like a stage-set. A gracious house full of "brittle beautiful things"—Kitty has "decorative genius"—and an atmosphere of comfort and ease where everything, even the crocuses along the drive, are planned and ordered. It would have been easy for the author to have introduced a note of satire from the very beginning at the expense of so much good taste and luxury. But the reader is drawn into the magic circle of Baldry Court and accepts Jenny, and even spoilt Kitty, who is associated only with delicate silken garments and rosebuds—even if she does look "so like a girl on a magazine cover that one expected to find a large '7d' somewhere attached to her person".

Into this exquisitely arranged Eden comes Margaret, with the news of Chris's condition and the revelation of his illusion: it is Margaret he wants to come home to, having blotted his marriage from his mind. To Kitty and Jenny it seemed inconceivable that Chris could ever have loved this plain, shabby woman, "repulsively furred with neglect and poverty", with her "deplorable umbrella, her unpardonable raincoat". Social snobbery is too flimsy a term for what they feel. Sexual jealousy and tribal instinct combine into hatred; Jenny "hated her as the rich hate the poor, as insect things that will struggle out of the crannies that are their decent home, and introduce ugliness to the light of day". For ugliness, at Baldry Court, is kept at bay by all the means that money and manner can muster. Margaret's intrusion was like "a spreading stain on the fabric of our life".

When Chris comes home and is faced with the unremembered Kitty, the thought of Margaret "made him unable to breathe, sent the blood running under his skin". Jenny, who is—though she never quite admits it—in love with Chris, feels "stunned with jealousy". "I suppose the truth is that I was physically so jealous of Margaret that it was making me ill." In *Henry James*, Rebecca West had written of the master's technique of significant omission: "that if one had a really 'great' scene one ought to leave it out and describe it simply by the full relation of its consequences". When Margaret is reunited with Chris in the garden of Baldry Court, Jenny watches from a top window, but covers her eyes so as not to witness their first embrace; and no one hears what they say. After, Jenny feels "utterly cut off" from Chris, and thinks of him "with the passion of exile". In his marriage to Kitty he had never thus excluded her. Now that he is regularly visited and comforted by Margaret, Kitty is like "a broken doll"; she "holds a review of her under-clothing", looking "wanly at the frail luminous silks" like a speculator who has cornered a commodity for which there is no demand.

Jenny, in spite of her jealousy, perceives Margaret's quality—

her simplicity, her serene, ecstatic goodness. She comes upon them in the woods—Chris peacefully sleeping, Margaret squatting protectively at his side—both "englobed in peace as in a crystal sphere". She feels that Margaret's "was the most significant as it was the loveliest attitude in the world":

> It means that the woman has gathered the soul of the man into her soul and is keeping it warm in love and peace so that his body can rest quiet for a little time. That is a great thing for a woman to do.

That may seem an unlikely opinion for the young, independent and feminist Rebecca West to endorse, as she surely does. What in fact she is celebrating is goodness, the creative, life-giving goodness that is independent of intellect, or of art as it is usually understood. The passage goes on:

> I know there are things at least as great for those women whose independent spirits can ride fearlessly and with interest outside the home park of their personal relationships, but independence is not the occupation of most of us. What we desire is greatness such as this which had given sleep to the beloved.

Rebecca West herself was one of the "independent spirits", but she has always had a robust and catholic understanding of creativity; the person who can make a good cake may be as creative as the person who can write a story. It is Margaret's self, her soul, that Chris loves. Jenny spells it out:

> I suppose that the subject of our tragedy, written in spiritual terms, was that in Kitty he had turned from the type of woman that makes the body conqueror of the soul and in me from the type that mediates between the soul and the body . . . and had given himself to a woman whose bleak habit it was to champion the soul against the body.

Kitty made the body "conqueror of the soul" only in one sense. She and Jenny were "images of Chris's conception of women": "Exquisite we were according to our equipment; unflushed by appetite or passion, even noble passion . . . and he had known none other than us. With such a mental habit a man could not help but wince at Margaret," thinks Jenny, wrongly as it happens. She is nearer the mark when she says, "we are as we are and there is nothing more to us. The whole truth about us is in our material seeming."

For in spite of their attractiveness she and Kitty are as passionless as flowers. Margaret, who "champions the soul against the body", can express her soul in a sexuality that answers Chris's own—his "body and soul were consumed with desire for her". When the Freudian doctor surmises that Chris turned to sex "with a peculiar need", it is Margaret who answers, to the discomfiture of the other two, "Yes, he was always very dependent."

One of Rebecca West's themes has been the sacrifice made by men (and therefore by society) of the sexual woman to the nonsexual woman. Here it comes about because it must. Margaret consents to cooperate in curing Chris—"making him ordinary", as she puts it—because the situation he so desires is not true. He was in reality married to Kitty, and Margaret was married to the dim Mr Grey. The world "will not suffer magic circles to endure". Truth must be faced at all costs. "I knew quite well," says Jenny, "that when one is adult one must raise to one's lips the wine of the truth . . . or else walk for ever queer and small like a dwarf." If Chris is allowed to stay in the magic circle of a past truth he "would not be quite a man". So by a heartbreaking device he is "cured", and walks back into his marriage with "a dreadful decent smile", "every inch a soldier".

Margaret, one imagines, in the dignity of a requited and renounced love, will continue to mother her husband. Jenny, the mediator, has reached new understanding. And Kitty, whom Jenny sees towards the end as "the falsest thing on earth, who was in tune with every kind of falsity", Rebecca West acknowledges, through Jenny, the role of all the Kitties of this world, watching her demeanour as she prepares to meet the new doctor. Kitty was "glowing", because she was going to meet a new man:

Beautiful women of her type lose, in this matter of admiration alone, their otherwise tremendous sense of class distinction; they are obscurely aware that it is their civilising mission to flash the jewel of their beauty before all men, so that they shall desire it and work to get the wealth to buy it, and thus be seduced by a present appetite to a tilling of the earth that serves the future. There is, you know, really room for all of us; we each have our peculiar use.

INTRODUCTION

In the last sentence of that quotation lies one of the characteristically ironic and characteristically humane illuminations that can be gleaned from *The Return of the Soldier*.

The sources of the novel are necessarily complex. Gordon N. Ray, in his *H. G. Wells and Rebecca West*, offers an interpretation that connects Kitty with Jane Wells. Rebecca West was living during the writing of the book in some anxiety and discomfort, and the ease and security of Baldry Court may well seem like a reflection of the ease and security—and perhaps the falsity—of Wells's domestic life. But she wrote to Ray on 14 July 1971 that although he had given "a most brilliant explanation", such thoughts had not been at the forefront of her mind:

> The story was written round the personality of Mrs Vernon, a very nice woman, who was our landlady at Claverton Street over several years. . . . She was the complete Margaret, and she had once been to Monkey Island on an unspecified occasion, which was of great importance to her, and speculations on what this might have been gave me the idea for the story. Kitty is not at all my idea of Jane. . . The original of Kitty was a woman I met only once, when someone took me to a house said to be the original of the house Galsworthy describes as being built by Bosinney for Soames in the Forsyte Saga.

The Monkey Island setting (on the Thames, near Bray) of the early idyll between Chris and Margaret was one that was well known to the author. In the descriptions in this book it is always dusk on Monkey Island when the young man and the girl meet: "In the liquefaction of colours which happens on a summer evening, when the green grass seemed like a precious fluid poured out on the earth and dripping over to the river, and the chestnut candles were no longer proud flowers . . . but just wet lights in the humid mass of the trees. . . . " Rebecca West has a painter's eye, and can trace the mood of landscape in words as effectively as a poet. To readers more used to her analytic trenchancy and her deflationary wit her lyrical writing may cause a subtle unease: it is like seeing a panther playing very tenderly with a butterfly.

She had been happy herself at the Monkey Island Inn, which she makes Margaret's home. H. G. Wells too had known the place since he was a boy, when he used to pay summer visits to his

INTRODUCTION

uncle at the Surly Hall Inn, half a mile down river. Chris in the novel walks through the fields to visit Margaret from an uncle's house: "From Uncle Ambrose's gates one took the fieldpath across the meadow. . . " The quarrel on which Chris and Margaret so disastrously part was about the over-familiarity of one "Bert Wells, nephew to Mr Wells who keeps the inn at Surly Hall". This was just a private joke, as perhaps was the Wellsian appearance of the doctor at the end of the novel: "He was a little man with winking blue eyes, a flushed and crumpled forehead, a little grey moustache that gave him the profile of an amiable cat, and a lively taste in spotted ties . . ."

These are superficialities, grace-notes, but illustrative of the ease with which the author manipulates material in a book that is prodigal of insights and observations that a lesser writer would have made more of: as in a glancing sketch, for example, of the way Chris would talk to a pretty visitor, with "that detached attention, such as an unmusical man pays to good music, which men of anchored attentions give to attractive women".

Samuel Hynes has rightly written that *The Return of the Soldier* is "a small masterpiece"; and added, "but it is more nearly a 'woman's novel' . . . than anything else Dame Rebecca wrote. . . For it comes too close to being *merely* a woman's novel, and so confirming the notions about women that exist in a man-governed world." The plot may lead one to that conclusion; but it is an inadequate reading of the book as a whole, which has sharp things to say about truth and falsity, about confronting reality, about different modes of love and about the nature of goodness. In her later work Dame Rebecca has tended to concentrate on a complementary topic, the nature of evil. But the really striking thing about *The Return of the Soldier* is the way in which the preoccupations and the convictions of the mature writer are already discernible in this short, dramatic and very readable piece of fiction written in her early twenties.

Victoria Glendinning, 1980

THE RETURN OF THE SOLDIER

I

"Ah, don't begin to fuss!" wailed Kitty; "if a woman began to worry in these days because her husband hadn't written to her for a fortnight——! Besides, if he'd been anywhere interesting, anywhere where the fighting was really hot, he'd have found some way of telling me instead of just leaving it as 'Somewhere in France.' He'll be all right."

We were sitting in the nursery. I had not meant to enter it again after the child's death, but I had come suddenly on Kitty as she slipped the key into the lock and had lingered to look in at the high room, so full of whiteness and clear colours,

so unendurably gay and familiar, which is
kept in all respects as though there were
still a child in the house. It was the first
lavish day of spring, and the sunlight was
pouring through the tall arched windows
and the flowered curtains so brightly that
in the old days a fat fist would certainly
have been raised to point out the new
translucent glories of the rose-buds; it was
lying in great pools on the blue cork floor
and the soft rugs, patterned with strange
beasts; and it threw dancing beams, that
should have been gravely watched for
hours, on the white paint and the blue
distempered walls. It fell on the rocking-
horse which had been Chris's idea of an
appropriate present for his year-old son
and showed what a fine fellow he was and
how tremendously dappled; it picked out
Mary and her little lamb on the chintz
ottoman. And along the mantelpiece,
under the loved print of the snarling tiger,
in attitudes that were at once angular and
relaxed—as though they were ready for

play at their master's pleasure but found it hard to keep from drowsing in this warm weather—sat the Teddy Bear and the chimpanzee and the woolly white dog and the black cat with the eyes that roll. Everything was there, except Oliver. I turned away so that I might not spy on Kitty revisiting her dead.

But she called after me:

"Come here, Jenny. I'm going to dry my hair."

And when I looked again I saw that her golden hair was all about her shoulders and that she wore over her frock a little silken jacket trimmed with rosebuds. She looked so like a girl on a magazine cover that one expected to find a large "7d." somewhere attached to her person. She had taken Nanny's big basket-chair from its place by the high chair and was pushing it over to the middle window.

"I always come in here when Emery has washed my hair; it's the sunniest room in the house. I wish Chris wouldn't have

11

it kept as a nursery when there's no chance——"

She sat down, swept her hair over the back of the chair into the sunlight, and held out to me her tortoise-shell hairbrush.

"Give it a brush now and then like a good soul. But be careful. Tortoise snaps so."

I took the brush and turned to the window, leaning my forehead against the glass and staring unobservantly at the view. You probably know the beauty of that view; for when Chris rebuilt Baldry Court after his marriage, he handed it over to architects who had not so much the wild eye of the artist as the knowing wink of the manicurist, and between them they massaged the dear old place into matter for innumerable photographs in the illustrated papers.

The house lies on the crest of Harrowweald, and from its windows the eye drops to miles of emerald pastureland lying wet and brilliant under a westward line of sleek hills blue with distance and distant woods, while nearer it ranges the suave decorum of the lawn and the Lebanon cedar whose branches are like darkness made palpable, and the minatory gauntnesses of the top-most pines in the wood that breaks down-ward, its bare boughs a close texture of browns and purples, from the pond on the hill's edge.

That day its beauty was an affront to me, because like most Englishwomen of my time I was wishing for the return of a soldier. Disregarding the national interest and everything except the keen prehensile gesture of our hearts towards him, I wanted to snatch my cousin Christopher from the wars and seal him in this green pleasantness his wife and I now looked upon. Of late I had had bad dreams about him. By night I saw Chris running across the brown rottenness of No Man's Land, starting back here because he trod upon a hand, not even looking there be-cause of the awfulness of an unburied head, and not till my dream was packed full of horror did I see him pitch forward on his knees as he reached safety—if it was that. For on the war-films I have seen men slip down as softly from the trench parapet, and none but the grimmer philosophers would say that they had reached safety by their fall. And when I escaped into wakefulness it was only to lie stiff and think of stories I had heard in the boyish voice, that rings indomitable yet has most of its gay notes flattened, of the modern subaltern.

"We were all of us in a barn one night, and a shell came along. My pal sang out, '*Help me, old man, I've got no legs!*' and I had to answer, '*I can't, old man, I've got no hands!*'"

Well, such are the dreams of Englishwomen to-day; I could not complain. But I wished for the return of our soldier.

So I said: "I wish we could hear from Chris. It is a fortnight since he wrote."

And then it was that Kitty wailed, "Ah,

don't begin to fuss," and bent over her image in her hand-mirror as one might bend for refreshment over scented flowers.

I tried to build about me such a little globe of ease as always ensphered her, and thought of all that remained good in our lives though Chris had gone. My eye followed the mellow brick of the garden wall through the trees, and I reflected that by the contriving of these gardens that lay, well-kept as a woman's hand, on the south side of the hill, Kitty and I had proved ourselves worthy of the past generation that had set the old house on this sunny ledge, overhanging and overhung by beauty. And we had done much for the new house.

I could send my mind creeping from room to room like a purring cat, rubbing itself against all the brittle beautiful things that we had either recovered from antiquity or dug from the obscure pits of modern craftsmanship, basking in the colour that glowed from all our solemnly

15

chosen fabrics with such pure intensity that it seemed to shed warmth like sunshine. Even now, when spending seemed a little disgraceful, I could think of that beauty with nothing but pride. I was sure that we were preserved from the reproach of luxury because we had made a fine place for Chris, one little part of the world that was, so far as surfaces could make it so, good enough for his amazing goodness.

Here we had nourished that surpassing amiability which was so habitual that one took it as one of his physical characteristics, and regarded any lapse into bad temper as a calamity startling as the breaking of a leg. Here we had made happiness inevitable for him. I could shut my eyes and think of innumerable proofs of how well we had succeeded, for there never was so visibly contented a man: the way he lingered with us in the mornings while the car throbbed at the door, delighting just in whatever way the weather looked in the familiar frame of things, how our rooms burned with many coloured brightness on the darkest winter day, how not the fieriest summertime could consume the cool wet leafy places of our garden; the way that in the midst of entertaining a great company he would smile secretly to us, as though he knew we would not cease in our task of refreshing him; and all that he did on the morning just a year ago, when he went to the front. . . .

First he had sat in the morning-room and talked and stared out on the lawn that already had the desolation of an empty stage although he had not yet gone; then broke off suddenly and went about the house, looking into many rooms. He went to the stables and looked at the horses and had the dogs brought out; he refrained from touching them or speaking to them, as though he felt himself already infected with the squalor of war and did not want to contaminate their bright physical well-being. Then he went to the edge of the wood and stood staring down into the clumps of dark-leaved rhododendra and the yellow tangle of last year's bracken and the cold winter black of the trees. (From this very window I had spied on him.) Then he moved broodingly back to the house to be with his wife until the moment of his going, when I stood with her on the steps to see him motor off to Waterloo.

He kissed us both; as he bent over me I noticed once again how his hair was of two colours, brown and gold. Then he got into the car, put on his Tommy air, and said, "So long! I'll write you from Berlin!" and as he spoke his head dropped back and he set a hard stare on the overarching house. That meant, I knew, that he loved the life he had lived with us and desired to carry with him to the dreary place of death and dirt the completest picture of everything about his home, on which his mind could brush when things were at their worst, as a man might finger an amulet through his shirt. This house, this life with us, was the core of his heart.

"If he could come back!" I said. "He was so happy here."

And Kitty answered: "He could not have been happier."

It was important that he should have been happy, for, you see, he was not like other city men. When we had played together as children in that wood he had always shown great faith in the imminence of the improbable. He thought that the birch tree would really stir and shrink and quicken into an enchanted princess, that he really was a Red Indian and that his disguise would suddenly fall from him at the right sundown, that at any moment a tiger might lift red fangs through the bracken; and he expected these things with a stronger motion of the imagination than the ordinary child's make-believe. And from a thousand intimations, from his occasional clear fixity

19

of gaze on good things as though they were about to dissolve into better, from the passionate anticipation with which he went to new countries or met new people, I was aware that this faith had persisted into his adult life.

He had exchanged his expectation of becoming a Red Indian for the equally wistful aspiration of becoming completely reconciled to life. It was his hopeless hope that some time he would have an experience that would act on his life like alchemy, turning to gold all the dark metals of events, and from that revelation he would go on his way rich with an inextinguishable joy.

There had been, of course, no chance of his ever getting it. Literally there wasn't room to swing a revelation in his crowded life. First of all, at his father's death, he had been obliged to take over a business that was weighted by the needs of a mob of female relatives who were all useless either in the old way with antimacassars or in the new way with golf clubs.

Then Kitty had come along and picked up his conception of normal expenditure and carelessly stretched it as a woman stretches a new glove on her hand. Then there had been the difficult task of learning to live after the death of his little son. It had lain on us, as the responsibility that gave us dignity, to compensate him for his lack of free adventure by arranging him a gracious life. But now, just because our performance had been so brilliantly adequate, how dreary was the empty stage. . . .

We were not, perhaps, specially contemptible women, because nothing could ever really become a part of our life until it had been referred to Chris's attention. I remember thinking, as the parlourmaid came in with a card on the tray, how little it mattered who had called and what flag of prettiness she flew, since there was no chance that Chris would come in and stand over her, his fairness red in the firelight, and show her that detached attention, such as an unmusical man pays to good music, which men of anchored affections give to attractive women.

Kitty read from the card, "'Mrs. William Grey, Mariposa, Ladysmith Road, Wealdstone.' I don't know anybody in Wealdstone." That is the name of the red suburban stain which fouls the fields three miles nearer London than Harrow-weald. One cannot now protect one's environment as one could in the old days. "Do I know her, Ward? Has she been here before?"

"Oh, no, ma'am." The parlourmaid smiled superciliously. "She said she had news for you." From her tone one could deduce an over-confidential explanation made by a shabby visitor while using the door mat almost too zealously.

Kitty pondered and said, "I'll come down." As the girl went she took up the amber hairpins from her lap and began

22

swathing her hair about her head. "Last year's fashion," she commented; "but I fancy it'll do for a person with that sort of address." She stood up and threw her little silk dressing-jacket over the rocking-horse. "I'm seeing her because she may need something, and I specially want to be kind to people while Chris is away. One wants to deserve well of Heaven."

For a minute she was aloof in radiance, but as we linked arms and went out into the corridor she became more mortal with a pout.

"The people that come breaking into one's nice quiet day," she moaned reproachfully, and as we came to the head of the broad staircase she leaned over the white balustrade to peer down on the hall, and squeezed my arm. "Look!" she whispered.

Just beneath us, on one of Kitty's prettiest chintz arm-chairs, sat a middle-aged woman. She wore a yellowish rain-coat and a black hat with plumes whose sticky straw had but lately been renovated by something out of a little bottle bought at the chemist's. She had rolled her black thread gloves into a ball on her lap, so that she could turn her grey alpaca skirt well above her muddy boots and adjust its brushbraid with a seamed red hand which looked even more horrible when she presently raised it to touch the glistening flowers of the pink azalea that stood on a table beside her.

Kitty shivered and muttered, "Let's get this over," and ran down the stairs. On the last step she paused and said with a conscientious sweetness, "Mrs. Grey?"

"Yes," answered the visitor.

She lifted to Kitty a sallow and relaxed face whose expression gave me a sharp, pitying pang of prepossession in her favour; it was beautiful that so plain a woman should so ardently rejoice in another's loveliness.

"Are you Mrs. Baldry?" she asked, almost as if she were glad about it, and stood up.

24

The bones of her cheap stays clicked as she moved. Well, she was not so bad. Her body was long and round and shapely and with a noble squareness of the shoulders; her fair hair curled diffidently about a good brow; her grey eyes, though they were remote, as if anything worth looking at in her life had kept a long way off, were full of tenderness; and though she was slender there was something about her of the wholesome endearing heaviness of the draught-ox or the big trusted dog. Yet she was bad enough. She was repulsively furred with neglect and poverty, as even a good glove that has dropped down behind a bed in a hotel and has lain undisturbed for a day or two is repulsive when the chambermaid retrieves it from the dust and fluff.

She flung at us as we sat down:

"My general is sister to your second housemaid."

It left us at a loss. "You've come about a reference?"

"Oh, no. I've had Gladys two years now, and I've always found her a very good girl. I want no reference." With her finger-nail she followed the burst seam of the dark pigskin purse that slid about on her shiny alpaca lap. "But girls talk, you know. You mustn't blame them. . . ."

She seemed to be caught in a thicket of embarrassment, and sat staring up at the azalea.

Kitty said, with the hardness of a woman who sees before her the curse of women's lives, a domestic row, that she took no interest in servants' gossip.

"Oh, it isn't"—her eyes brimmed as though we had been unkind—"servants' gossip that I wanted to talk about. I only mentioned Gladys"—she continued to trace the burst seam of her purse—"because that's how I heard you didn't know."

"What don't I know?"

Her head dropped a little.

26

"About Mr. Baldry. Forgive me, I don't know his rank."

"Captain Baldry," supplied Kitty wonderingly. "What is it that I don't know about him?"

She looked far away from us, to the open door and its view of dark pines and pale March sunshine, and appeared to swallow something.

"Why, that he's hurt," she gently said.

"Wounded, you mean?" asked Kitty.

Her rusty plumes oscillated as she moved her mild face about with an air of perplexity.

"Yes," she said, "he's wounded."

Kitty's bright eyes met mine and we obeyed that mysterious human impulse to smile triumphantly at the spectacle of a fellow-creature occupied in baseness. For this news was not true. It could not possibly be true. The War Office would have wired to us immediately if Chris had been wounded. This was such a fraud as one sees recorded in the papers that meticulously record squalor, in paragraphs headed "Heartless Fraud on Soldier's Wife."

Presently she would say that she had gone to some expense to come here with her news, and that she was poor, and at the first generous look on our faces there would come some tale of trouble that would disgust the imagination by pictures of yellow wood furniture that a landlord oddly desired to seize and a pallid child with bandages round its throat.

I turned away my eyes and tried to be inattentive. Yet there was something about the physical quality of the woman, unlovely though she was, which preserved the occasion from utter baseness. I felt sure that had it not been for the tyrannous emptiness of that evil, shiny, pigskin purse that jerked about on her trembling knees, the poor driven creature would have chosen ways of candour and gentleness. It was, strangely enough, only when I looked at Kitty and marked how her brightly

28

coloured prettiness arched over this plain criminal, as though she were a splendid bird of prey and this her sluggish insect food, that I felt the moment degrading.

She was, I felt, being a little too clever over it.

"How is he wounded?" she asked.

The caller traced a pattern on the carpet with her blunt toe.

"I don't know how to put it. . . . He's not exactly wounded. . . . A shell burst. . . ."

"Concussion?" suggested Kitty.

She answered with an odd glibness and humility, as though tendering us a term she had long brooded over without arriving at comprehension, and hoping that our superior intelligences would make something of it. "Shell-shock." Our faces did not illumine so she dragged on lamely. "Anyway, he's not well." Again she played with her purse. Her face was visibly damp.

"Not well? Is he dangerously ill?"

29

"Oh, no!" She was too kind to harrow us. "Not dangerously ill."

Kitty brutally permitted a silence to fall. Our caller could not bear it, and broke it in a voice that nervousness had turned to a funny diffident croak.

"He's in the Queen Mary Hospital at Boulogne." We did not speak, and she began to flush and wriggle on her seat, and stooped forward to fumble under the legs of her chair for her umbrella. The sight of its green seams and unveracious tortoise-shell handle disgusted Kitty into speech.

"How do you know all this?"

Our visitor met her eyes. This was evidently a moment for which she had steeled herself, and she rose to it with a catch of her breath.

"A man who used to be a clerk along with my husband is in Mr. Baldry's regiment." Her voice croaked even more piteously and her eyes begged, "Leave it at that! Leave it at that! If you only knew——"

"And what regiment is that?" pursued Kitty.

The poor sallow face shone with sweat.

"I never thought to ask!" she said.

"Well, your friend's name. . . ."

Mrs. Grey moved on her seat so suddenly and violently that the pigskin purse fell from her lap and lay at my feet. I supposed that she cast it from her purposely because its emptiness had brought her to this humiliation, and that the scene would close presently in a few quiet tears.

I hoped that Kitty would let her go without scaring her too much with words and would not mind if I gave her a little money. There was no doubt in my mind but that this queer ugly episode, in which this woman butted like a clumsy animal at a gate she was not intelligent enough to open, would dissolve and be replaced by some more pleasing composition in which we would take our proper parts; in which, that is, she should turn from our rightness ashamed.

Yet she cried, "But Chris is ill!"

It took a second for the compact insolence of the moment to penetrate: the amazing impertinence of the use of his name, the accusation of callousness she brought against us, whose passion for Chris was our point of honour, because we would not shriek at her false news, the impudently bright indignant gaze she flung at us, the lift of her voice that pretended she could not understand our coolness and irrelevance.

I pushed the purse away from me with my toe and hated her as the rich hate the poor, as insect things that will struggle out of the crannies which are their decent home, and introduce ugliness to the light of day. And Kitty said, in a voice shaken with pitilessness:

"You are impertinent. I know exactly what you are doing. You have read in the *Harrow Observer* or somewhere that my husband is at the front, and you come to tell this story because you think

that you will get some money. I've read
of such cases in the papers. You forget
that if anything has happened to my
husband the War Office would have told
me. You should think yourself very lucky
that I don't hand you over to the police."
She shrilled a little before she came to the
end. "Please go!"

"Kitty!" I breathed.

I was so ashamed that such a scene
should spring from Chris's peril at the
front that I wanted to go out into the
garden and sit by the pond until the poor
thing had removed her deplorable umbrella, her unpardonable raincoat, her
poor frustrated fraud. But Mrs. Grey,
who had begun, childishly and deliber-
ately, "It's *you* who are being . . ." and
had desisted, simply because she realized
that there were no harsh notes on her lyre
and that she could not strike these chords
that others found so easy, had fixed me
with a certain wet, clear, patient gaze.
It is the gift of animals and those of

peasant stock. From the least regarded, from an old horse nosing over a gate or a drab in a workhouse ward, it wrings the heart. From this woman . . . I said checkingly, "Kitty!" and reconciled her in an undertone ("There's some mistake. Got the name wrong, perhaps). Please tell us all about it, Mrs. Grey."

Mrs. Grey began a forward movement like a curtsey. She was grovelling after that purse. When she rose her face was pink from stooping and her dignity swam uncertainly in a sea of half-shed tears. She said:

"I'm sorry I've upset you. But when you know a thing like that it isn't in flesh and blood to keep it from his wife. I am a married woman myself and I know. I knew Mr. Baldry fifteen years ago." Her voice freely confessed that she had taken a liberty. "Quite a friend of the family he was." She had added that touch to soften the crude surprisingness of her announcement. It hardly did. "We lost sight of each other. It's fifteen years since we last met. I had never seen or heard of him, nor thought to do again till I got this a week ago."

She undid the purse and took out a telegram. I knew suddenly that all she said was true; for that was why her hands had clasped that purse.

"He isn't well! He isn't well!" she said pleadingly. "He's lost his memory, and thinks—thinks he still knows me."

She passed the telegram to Kitty, who read it and laid it on her knee.

"See," said Mrs. Grey, "it's addressed to Margaret Allington, my maiden name, and I've been married these ten years. And it was sent to my old home, Monkey Island at Bray. Father kept the inn there. It's fifteen years since we left it. I never should have got this telegram if me and my husband hadn't been down there a little while back and told the folks who keep it now who I was."

Kitty folded up the telegram and said in a little voice:

"This is a likely story."

Again her grey eyes brimmed. People are rude to one, she visibly said, but surely not nice people like this. She simply continued to sit.

Kitty cried out, as though arguing:

"There's nothing about shell-shock in this wire."

She melted into a trembling shyness.

"There was a letter too."

Kitty held out her hand.

She gasped. "Oh, no! I couldn't do that."

"I must have it," said Kitty.

The caller's eyes grew great, she rose and dived clumsily for her umbrella, which had again slipped under the chair. "I can't," she cried, and scurried to the open door like a pelted dog. She would have run down the steps at once had not some tender thought arrested her. She turned to me trustfully and stammered, "He is at that hospital I said," as if, since I had dealt her no direct blow, I might be able to salve the news she brought from the general wreck of manners. And then Kitty's stiff pallor struck to her heart, and she cried comfortingly across the distance, "But I tell you I haven't seen him for fifteen years." She faced about, pushed down her hat on her head, and ran down the steps on to the gravel. "They won't understand," we heard her sob.

For a long time we watched her as she went along the drive, her yellowish rain-coat looking sick and bright in the sharp sunshine, her black plumes nodding like the pines above, her cheap boots making her walk on her heels; a spreading stain on the fabric of our life. When she was quite hidden by the dark clump of rhodo-dendra at the corner Kitty turned and went to the fire-place. She laid her arms against the oak mantelpiece and cooled her face against her arms.

When at last I followed her she said,

"Do you believe her?"

I started. I had forgotten that we had ever disbelieved her.

"Yes."

"What can it mean?" She dropped her arms and stared at me imploringly. "Think, think of something it can mean which isn't detestable!"

"It's all a mystery," I said; and added mildly, because nobody has ever been cross with Kitty, "You didn't help to clear it up."

"Oh, I know you think I was rude," she petulantly moaned, "but you're so slow, you don't see what it means. Either it means that he's mad, our Chris, our splendid sane Chris, all broken and queer, not knowing us. . . . I can't bear to think of that. It can't be true. But if he isn't . . . Jenny, there was nothing in that telegram to show he'd lost his memory. It was just affection—a name that might have been a pet name—things that it was a little common to put in a telegram. It's queer he should have written such a message, queer that he shouldn't have told me about knowing her, queer that he ever should have known such a woman. It shows there are bits of him we don't know. Things may be awfully wrong. It's all such a breach of trust. I resent it."

I was appalled by this stiff dignified gesture that seemed to be plucking Chris's soul from his body. She was hurt, of course. But there are ways pain should not show itself. . . .

"But Chris is ill," I said.

She stared at me. "You're saying what she said."

Indeed there seemed no better words than those Mrs. Grey had used. I repeated. "But he is ill."

She laid her face against her arms again. "What does that matter?" she said. "If he could send that telegram, he. . . ." She paused, breathed deeply, and went on with the sick delight the unhappy sometimes find in ungraciousness. "If he could send that telegram he isn't ours any longer."

II

I was sorry, the next morning, that the post comes too late at Harrow-weald to be brought up with the morning tea and waits for one at the breakfast table; for under Kitty's fixed gaze I had to open a letter which bore the Boulogne postmark and was addressed in the writing of Frank Baldry, Chris's cousin, who is in the Church.

"Dear Jenny," it began, "I am sorry to have to tell you that poor Chris has been disabled. He has had shell-shock and although not physically wounded is in a very strange state indeed. I got a wire from him on Thursday saying he was in hospital about a mile from Boulogne and that he wanted to see me. The telegram had not been sent direct to me, but to Ollenshaws, although I left the Ollenshaws curacy for Pentmouth nearly fifteen years ago. Sumpter is still there, luckily, and forwarded it on at once. I started that evening and looked hard for you and Kitty on the boat, naturally expecting to see you. But as you now know you were not there. I found the hospital in a girl's school which had been taken over by the Red Cross. The Red Cross is everywhere here.

"I found Chris in a nice room with a southern exposure with three other officers, who seemed very decent. He was better than I had expected but did not look quite himself. For one thing he was oddly boisterous in his greeting. He seemed glad to see me, and told me he could remember nothing about his concussion, but that he wanted to get back to Harrow-weald. He said things about the wood and the upper pond that seemed sentimental but not so much out of the way. He wanted to know if the daffies

41

were out yet, and when he would be
allowed to travel, because he felt that he
would get well at once if only he could
get home. And then he was silent for a
minute as though he was holding something
back. When he did begin to let out what
he was holding back I was amazed. I
will try and set it down as far as possible
in the order in which it occurs. He in-
formed me—with just the boyish manner
he might have used fifteen years ago—
that he was in love with a girl called
Margaret Allington, who is the daughter
of the man who keeps the inn on Monkey
Island at Bray on the Thames. I gasped,
'How long has this been going on?' He
laughed at my surprise, and said, 'Ever
since I went down to stay with Uncle
Ambrose at Dorney after I'd got my
degree.' Fifteen years ago! I was still
staring at him, unable to believe this bare-
faced admission of a deception carried on
for years, when he went on to say that
though he had wired to her and she had

wired a message in return, she hadn't said anything about coming over to see him. 'Now,' he said quite coolly, 'I know old Allington's had a bad season—oh, I'm quite well up in the innkeeping business these days!—and I think it may quite possibly be a lack of funds that is keeping her away. I've lost my cheque-book somewhere in the scrim and so I wonder if you'd send her some money. Or better still, for she's a shy country thing, you might fetch her.'

"I stared. 'Chris,' I said, 'I know the war is making some of us very lax, and nobody could be more broadminded than I am. But there are limits. And when it comes to asking me to go over to England and fetch a woman. . . .' He interrupted me with a sneer that we parsons are inveterately eighteenth century and have our minds perpetually inflamed by visions of squires' sons seducing country wenches, and declared that he meant to marry this Margaret Allington. 'Oh, indeed,' I said. 'And may I ask what Kitty says to this arrangement?' 'Who the devil is Kitty?' he asked blankly. 'Kitty is your wife,' I said quietly, but firmly. He sat up and exclaimed, 'I haven't got a wife! Has some woman been turning up with a cock-and-bull story of being my wife? Because it's the damnedest lie!'

"I determined to settle the matter by sharp common-sense handling. 'Chris,' I said, 'you have evidently lost your memory. You were married to Kitty Ellis at St. George's, Hanover Square, on the third, or it may have been the fourth'—you know my wretched memory for dates—'of February in 1906.' He turned very pale and asked what year this was. '1916,' I told him. He fell back in a fainting condition. The nurse came and said I had done it all right this time, so she at least seemed to have known that he required a rude awakening, although the doctor (a very nice man,

Winchester and New) told me he had known nothing of Chris's delusions.

"An hour later I was called back into the room. Chris was looking at himself in a hand mirror, which he threw on the floor as I entered. 'You arc right,' he said. 'I'm not twenty-one, but thirty-six.' He said he felt lonely and afraid, and that I must bring Margaret Allington to him at once or he would die. Suddenly he stopped raving and asked, 'Is Father all right?' I prayed for guidance and answered, 'Your father passed away twelve years ago.' He said, 'Good God, can't you say he *died?*' and he turned over and lay with his back to me. I have never before seen a strong man weep and it is indeed a terrible sight. He moaned a lot and began to call for this Margaret. Then he turned over again and said 'Now tell us all about this Kitty that I've married.' I told him she was a beautiful little woman and mentioned that she had a charming and cultivated soprano voice. He said very fractiously, 'I don't like little women and I hate everybody, male or female, who sings. O God, I don't like this Kitty. Take her away.' And then he began to rave again about this woman. He said that his body and soul were consumed with desire for her and that he would never rest until he once more held her in his arms. I had no suspicion that Chris had this side to his nature and it was almost a relief when he fainted again.

"I have seen him since and it is evening. But I have had a long talk with the doctor, who says that he has satisfied himself that Chris is suffering from a loss of memory extending over a period of fifteen years. He says that though of course it will be an occasion of great trial to us all he thinks that in view of Chris's expressed longing for Harrowweald he ought to be taken home, and advises me to make all arrangements for bringing him back some time next week. I hope I shall be upheld in this difficult enterprise.

"In the meantime I leave it to you to prepare Kitty for this terrible shock. How to do that you will know better than I. I wish she could be spared the experience, but since he is coming back and is certain to betray his real forgetfulness of her—for I am convinced there is no shamming in the business, there is a real gap in his memory—she must of course be made to understand. I hope she may have strength in the time of trial that lies before her and if I can be of any help to her no one will be more glad than I to render it. Tell me if I can run over now or any time either to talk to her or to help, so far as I can help, with him. You know how much I have always cared for dear old Chris. Yours ever, FRANK."

Over my shoulder Kitty muttered, "And he always pretended he liked my singing. . . ." And then gripped my arm and cried in a possessive fury. "Bring him home! Bring him home!"

And so, a week later, they brought Chris home.

From breakfast-time that day the house was pervaded with a day-before-the-funeral feeling: although all duties arising from the occasion had been performed one could settle to nothing else. Chris was expected at one, but there then came a telegram to say he was delayed till the late afternoon. So Kitty, whose beauty was as changed in grief from its ordinary seeming as a rose in moonlight is different from a rose by day, took me down after lunch to the greenhouses and had a snappishly competent conversation about the year's vegetables with Pipe the gardener. After she had said many such horticulturally scandalous things as "I know Queen Mary's prolific, but she isn't sweet," she tugged at my hand and we went back to the house and found a great piece of the afternoon still on our hands. So Kitty went into the drawing-room and filled the house with the desolate merriment of

48

an inattentively played pianola while I sat in the hall and wrote letters and noticed how sad dance music has sounded ever since the war began. And then she started a savage raid of domestic efficiency and made the housemaids cry because the brass handles of the tallboys were not bright enough and because there was only a ten to one instead of a hundred to one risk of breaking a leg on the parquet. After that she had tea, and hated the soda-cake. She was a little shrunk thing, huddled in the arm-chair farthest from the light, when at last the big car came nosing up the drive through the dusk.

We stood up. Through the thudding of the engines came the sound of Chris's great male voice, that always had in it a note like the baying of a big dog. *"Thanks, I can manage by myself. . . ."* I heard, amazed, his step ring strong upon the stone, for I had felt his absence as a kind of death from which he would emerge ghostlike impalpable. And then he stood in the doorway, the gloom blurring his outlines like fur, the faint clear candlelight catching the fair down on his face. He did not see me, in my dark dress, nor huddled Kitty, and with the sleepy smile of one who returns to a dear familiar place to rest, he walked into the hall and laid down his stick and his khaki cap beside the candlestick on the oak table. With both his hands he felt the old wood and stood humming happily through his teeth.

I cried out, because I had seen that his hair was of three colours now—brown and gold and silver.

With a quick turn of the head he found me out in the shadows. "Hullo, Jenny!" he said, and gripped my hands.

"Oh, Chris, I am so glad," I stuttered, and then could say no more for shame that I was thirty-five instead of twenty. For his eyes had hardened in the midst of his welcome as though he had trusted

50

that I at least would have been no party to this conspiracy to deny that he was young, and he said: "I've dropped Frank in town. My temper's of the convalescent type." He might as well have said, "I've dropped Frank, who has grown old, like you. . . ."

"Chris," I went on, "it's so wonderful to have you safe. . . ."

"Safe," he repeated. He sighed very deeply and continued to hold my hands. There was a rustle in the shadows, and he dropped my hands.

The face that looked out of the dimness to him was very white; her upper lip was lifted over her teeth in a distressed grimace. And it was immediately as plain as though he had shouted it that this sad mask meant nothing to him. He knew, not because memory had given him any insight into her heart but because there is an instinctive kindliness in him which makes him wise about all suffering, that it would hurt her if he asked if this was his wife, but his body involuntarily began a gesture of inquiry before he realized that that too would hurt her and he checked it half-way. So, through a silence, he stood before her slightly bent, as though he had been maimed.

"I am your wife." There was a weak, wailing anger behind the words.

"Kitty," he said, softly and kindly. He looked round for some graciousness to make the scene less wounding, and stooped to kiss her. But he could not. The thought of another woman made him unable to breathe, sent the blood running under his skin.

With a toss, like a child saying, "Well, if you don't want to, I'm sure I wouldn't for the world!" Kitty withdrew from the suspended caress. He watched her retreat into the shadows, as though she were a symbol of this new life by which he was baffled and oppressed, until the darkness outside became filled with the sound like the surf which we always hear at Harrowweald on angry evenings, and his eyes became distant and his lips smiled. "Up here . . . in this old place . . . how one hears the pines. . . ."

She cried out from the other end of the room, as though she were speaking with someone behind a shut door. "I've ordered dinner at seven. I thought you'd probably have missed a meal or two. Or would want to go to bed early." She said it very smartly, with her head on one side like a bird, as if she was pleading that he would find her very clever about ordering dinner and thinking of his comfort.

"Good," he said. "I'd better dress now, hadn't I?" He looked up the staircase and would have gone up had I not held him back. For the little room in the south wing with the fishing-rods and the old books went in the rebuilding, absorbed by the black and white magnificence that is Kitty's bedroom.

"Oh, I'll take you up!" Kitty rang out efficiently. She pulled at his coat

sleeve, so they started level on the lowest
step. But as they went up the sense of
his separateness beat her back; she lifted
her arms as though she struggled through
a fog, and fell behind. When he reached
the top she was standing half-way down
the stairs, her hands clasped under her
chin. But he did not see her. He was
looking along the corridor and saying,
"This house is different." If the soul
has to stay in its coffin till the lead is
struck asunder, in its captivity it speaks
with such a voice.

She braced herself with a gallant laugh.
"How you've forgotten," she cried, and
ran up to him, rattling her keys and looking grave with housewifery, and I was
left alone with the dusk and the familiar
things. The dusk flowed in wet and cool
from the garden as if to put out the fire
of confusion lit on our hearthstone, and
the furniture, very visible through the
soft evening opacity with the observant
brightness of old well-polished wood,

seemed terribly aware. Strangeness had
come into the house and everything was
appalled by it, even time. For the
moments dragged. It seemed to me, half
an hour later, that I had been standing
for an infinite period in the drawing-
room, remembering that in the old days
the blinds had never been drawn in this
room because old Mrs. Baldry had liked
to see the night gathering like a pool in
the valley while the day lingered as a
white streak above the farthest hills; and
perceiving in pain that the heavy blue
blinds, which shroud the nine windows
because a lost Zeppelin sometimes clanks
like a skeleton across the sky above us,
would make his home seem even more
like prison.

I began to say what was in my mind
to Kitty when she came in, but she
moved past me, remote in preoccupation,
and I was silent when I saw that she was
dressed in all respects like a bride. The
gown she wore on her wedding-day ten

55

years ago had been cut and embroidered
as this white satin was, her hair had been
coiled low on her neck as it was now.
Around her throat were her pearls, and
her longer chain of diamonds dropped,
looking cruelly bright, to her white small
breasts; because she held some needle-
work to her bosom I saw that her right
hand was stiff with rings and her left hand
bare save for her wedding-ring. She
dropped her load of flannel on a work-
table and sat down, spreading out her
skirts, in an arm-chair by the fire. With
her lower lip thrust out, as if she were
considering a menu, she lowered her head
and looked down on herself. She frowned
to see that the high lights on the satin
shone scarlet from the fire, that her flesh
glowed like a rose, and she changed her
seat for a high-backed chair beneath the
furthest candle sconce. There were green
curtains close by, and now the lights on
her satin gown were green like cleft ice.
She looked cold as moonlight, as virginity,

but precious; the falling candlelight struck her hair to bright, pure gold. So she waited for him.

There came suddenly a thud at the door. We heard Chris swear and stumble to his feet, while one of the servants spoke helpfully. Kitty knitted her brows, for she hates gracelessness and a failure of physical adjustment is the worst indignity she can conceive. "He's fallen down those three steps from the hall," I whispered. "They're new. . . ." She did not listen, because she was controlling her face into harmony with the appearance of serene virginity upon which his eyes would light when he entered the room.

His fall had ruffled him and made him look very large and red, and he breathed hard like an animal pursued into a strange place by night, and to his hot consciousness of his disorder the sight of Kitty, her face and hands and bosom shining like the snow, her gown enfolding her and her gold hair crowning her with radiance and the white fire of jewels giving a passion to the spectacle, was a deep refreshment. She sat still for a time, so that he might feel this well. Then raised her ringed hand to her necklaces.

"It seems so strange that you should not remember me," she said. "You gave me all these."

He answered kindly. "I am glad I did that. You look very beautiful in them." But as he spoke his gaze shifted to the shadows in the corners of the room. He was thinking of another woman, of another beauty.

Kitty put up her hands as if to defend her jewels.

In that silence dinner was announced, and we went into the dining-room. It is the fashion at Baldry Court to use no electric light save when there is work to be done or a great company to be entertained, and to eat and talk by the mild clarity of many candles. That night it was a kindly fashion, for we sat about

58

the table with our faces veiled in shadow and seemed to listen in quiet contentment to the talk of our man who had come back to us. Yet all through the meal I was near to weeping because whenever he thought himself unobserved he looked at the things that were familiar to him. Dipping his head he would glance sideways at the old oak panelling; and nearer things he fingered as though sight were not intimate enough a contact, his hand caressed the arm of his chair, because he remembered the black gleam of it, stole out and touched the recollected salt-cellar. It was his furtiveness that was heartrending; it was as though he were an outcast and we who loved him stout policemen. Was Baldry Court so sleek a place that the unhappy felt offenders there? Then we had all been living wickedly and he too. As his fingers glided here and there he talked bravely about noncommittal things; to what ponies we had been strapped when at the age of

five we were introduced to the hunting-
field; how we had teased to be allowed
to keep swans in the pond above the
wood, and how the yellow bills of our
intended pets had sent us shrieking home-
wards; and all the dear life that makes
the bland English countryside so secretly
adventurous. "Funny thing," he said,
"All the time I was at Boulogne I wanted
to see a kingfisher. That blue, scudding
down a stream. Or a heron's flight round
a willow." . . . He checked himself suddenly; his head fell forward on his chest.
"You have no herons here, of course,"
he said drearily, and fingered the arm of
his chair again. Then raised his head
again, brisk with another subject. "Do
they still have trouble with foxes at
Steppy End?"

Kitty shook her head. "I don't
know. . . ."

"Griffiths will know," Chris said cheerily
and swung round on his seat to ask
the butler, and found him osseous where

Griffiths was rotund, dark where Griffiths had been merrily mottled, strange where Griffiths had been a part of home, a condition of life. He sat back in his chair as though his heart had stopped.

When the butler who is not Griffiths had left the room he spoke gruffly.

"Stupid of me, I know. But where is Griffiths?"

"Dead seven years ago," said Kitty, her eyes on her plate.

He sighed deeply in a shuddering horror. "I'm sorry. He was a good man."

I cleared my throat. "There are new people here, Chris, but they love you as the old ones did."

He forced himself to smile at us both, to a gay response. "As if I didn't know that to-night!"

But he did not know it. Even to me he would give no trust, because it was Jenny the girl who had been his friend and not Jenny the woman. All the inhabitants of this new tract of time were

61

his enemies, all its circumstances his prison bars. There was suspicion in his gesture with which, when we were back in the drawing-room, he picked up the flannel from the work-table.

"Whose is this?" he said curiously; his mother had been a hard riding woman, not apt with her needle.

"Clothes for one of the cottagers," answered Kitty breathlessly. "We— we've a lot of responsibilities, you and I. With all the land you've bought there's ever so many people to look after. . . ."

He moved his shoulders uneasily, as if under a yoke, and after he had drunk his coffee pulled up one of the blinds and went out to pace the flagged walk under the windows. Kitty huddled carelessly by the fire, her hands over her face, unheeding that by its red glow she looked not so virginal and bridelike, so I think she was too distracted even to plan. I went to the piano. Through this evening of sentences cut short because their completed meaning was always sorrow, of normal life dissolved to tears, the chords of Beethoven sounded serenely.

"So like you, Jenny," said Kitty suddenly, "to play Beethoven when it's the war that's caused all this. I could have told that you would have chosen to play German music, this night of all nights."

So I began a sarabande by Purcell, a jolly thing that makes one see a plump, sound woman dancing on a sanded floor in some old inn with casks of good ale all about her and a world of sunshine and May lanes without. As I played I wondered if things like this happened when Purcell wrote such music, empty of everything except laughter' and simple greeds and satisfactions and at the worst the wail of unrequited love. Why had modern life brought forth these horrors that make the old tragedies seem no more than nursery shows? Perhaps it is that adventurous men have too greatly changed the outward world which is life's engender-

ment. There are towns now, and even
the trees and flowers are not as they were;
the crocuses on the lawn, whose blades
showed white in the wide beam let out
by the window Chris had opened, should
have pierced turf on Mediterranean cliffs;
the golden larch beyond should have cast
its long shadows on little yellow men as
they crossed a Chinese plain. And the
sky also is different. Behind Chris's head,
as he halted at the open window, a searchlight turned all ways in the night like a
sword brandished among the stars.

"Kitty."

"Yes, Chris." She was sweet and
obedient and alert.

"I know my conduct must seem to
you perversely insulting." Behind him
the searchlight wheeled while he gripped
the sides of the window. "But if I do
not see Margaret Allington I shall die."

She raised her hands to her jewels
and pressed the cool globes of her pearls
into her flesh. "She lives near here,"

she said easily. "I will send the car down for her to-morrow. You shall see as much of her as you like."

His arms fell to his side. "Thank you," he muttered. "You're all being so kind——" he disengaged himself into the darkness.

I was amazed at Kitty's beautiful act and more amazed to find that it had made her face ugly. Her eyes snapped as they met mine. "That dowd!" she said, keeping her voice low so that he might not hear it as he passed to and fro before the window. "That dowd!"

This sudden abandonment of beauty and amiability means so much in our Kitty, whose law of life is grace, that I went over and kissed her. "Dear, you're taking things all the wrong way," I said. "Chris is ill——"

"He's well enough to remember her all right,". she replied unanswerably.

Her silver shoe tapped the floor, she pinched her lips for some moments. "After

65

all, I suppose I can sit down to it. Other women do. Teddy Rex keeps a Gaiety girl and Mrs. Rex has to grin and bear it."

She shrugged in answer to my silence. "What else is it, do you think? It means that Chris is a man like other men. But I did think that bad women were pretty. I suppose he's had so much to do with pretty ones that a plain one's a change. . . ."

"Kitty! Kitty! how can you?" But her little pink mouth went on manufacturing malice. "This is all a blind," she said at the end of an unpardonable sentence. "He's pretending. . . ." I was past speech then, who had felt his agony all the evening like a wound in my own body, and I did not care what I did to stop her. I gripped her small shoulders with my large hands and shook her till her jewels rattled and she scratched my fingers and gasped for breath. But I did not mind so long as she was silent.

Chris spoke from the darkness. "Jenny!"

I let her go. He came in and stood over us, running his hand through his hair unhappily. "Let's all be decent to each other," he said heavily. "It's all such a muddle and it's so rotten for all of us. . . ."

Kitty shook herself neat and stood up. "Why don't you say, 'Jenny, you mustn't be rude to visitors?' It's how you feel, I know." She gathered up her needle-work. "I'm going to bed. It's been a horrid night."

She spoke so pathetically, like a child who hasn't enjoyed a party as much as it had thought it would, that both of us felt a stir of tenderness towards her as she left the room. We smiled sadly at each other as we sat down by the fire, and I perceived that, perhaps because I was flushed and looked younger, he felt more intimate with me than he had yet done since his return. Indeed in the warm friendly silence that followed he was like

a patient when tiring visitors have gone
and he is left alone with his trusted nurse;
smiled under drooped lids and then paid
me the high compliment of disregard.
His limbs relaxed, he sank back into his
chair. I watched him vigilantly and was
ready at that moment when thought
intruded into his drowsings and his face
began to twitch.

"You can't remember her at all?" I
asked.

"Oh, yes," he said, without raising his
eyelids. "In a sense. I know how she
bows when you meet her in the street,
how she dresses when she goes to church.
I know her as one knows a woman staying
in the same hotel. Just like that."

"It's a pity you can't remember Kitty
All that a wife should be she's been to
you."

He sat forward, warming his palms at
the blaze and hunching his shoulders as
though there was a draught. His silence
compelled me to look at him and I found

his eyes on me, cold and incredulous and frightened. "Jenny, is this true?"

"That Kitty's been a good wife?"

"That Kitty is my wife. That I am old. That——" he waved a hand at the altered room—"all this."

"It is all true. She is your wife and this place is changed—and it's better and jollier in all sorts of ways, believe me— and fifteen years have passed. Why, Chris, can't you see that I have grown old?" My vanity could hardly endure his slow stare but I kept my fingers clasped on my lap. "You see?"

He turned away with an assenting mutter. But I saw that deep down in him, not to be moved by any material proof, his spirit was incredulous.

"Tell me what seems real to you," I begged. "Chris, be a pal—I'll never tell——"

"Mmm," he said. His elbows were on his knees, and his hands stroked his thick tarnished hair; I could not see his face, but I knew that his skin was red and that his grey eyes were wet and bright. Then suddenly he lifted his chin and laughed, like a happy swimmer breaking through a wave that has swept him far inshore. He glowed with a radiance that illuminated the moment till my blood tingled and I began to run my hands together and laugh too. "Why, Monkey Island's real. But you don't know old Monkey. Let me tell you——"

I have lived so long with the story which he told me that I cannot now remember his shy phrases. But this is how I have visualized his meeting with love on his secret island. I think it is the truth.

III

From Uncle Ambrose's gates one took the
field-path across the meadow where Whis-
ton's cows are put to graze and got through
the second stile, the one between the two
big alders, into a long straight road that
ran, very tedious in the trough of hot
air that is the Thames valley, across the
flat lands to Bray. After a mile or so
there branched from it a private road
which followed a line of noble poplars
that led to the pretentiously simple porch
of a *cottage ornée* called "The Hut." One
passed that and went on to a group of
outbuildings which gave, as it seemed
impossible that bricks and wood and
plaster should give, an impression that
they were knock-kneed. There was a
shed that let in the rain through its mossy
tiles and sported a board "Garage"; there

was a glasshouse containing a pinched and sulky vine; there was a hasty collection of planks set askew over an agricultural machine of some sort; there were three barrels of concrete and an empty and rusting aviary. "Margaret's father," said Chris, "had bought them at sales." Past these marched the poplars and lifted their strong yet tremulous silver spires on each side of the gravel slope which went down to the ferry; between two of them—he described it meticulously as though it were of immense significance—there stood a white hawthorn. In front were the dark green glassy waters of an unvisited backwater; and beyond them a bright lawn set with many walnut trees and a few great chestnuts, well lit with their candles, and to the left of that a low white house with a green dome rising in its middle and a veranda whose roof of hammered iron had gone verdigris colour with age and the Thames weather. This was the Monkey Island Inn. The third Duke of Marlborough had built it for a "folly," and perching there with nothing but a line of walnut trees and a fringe of lawn between it and the fast full shining Thames it had a grace and silliness that belonged to the eighteenth century.

Well, one sounded the bell that hung on a post, and presently Margaret in a white dress would come out of the porch and would walk to the stone steps down to the river. Invariably, as she passed the walnut tree that overhung the path, she would pick a leaf and crush it and sniff the sweet scent; and as she came near the steps she would shade her eyes and peer across the water. "She is a little near-sighted; you can't imagine how sweet it makes her look." (I did not say that I had seen her, for indeed this Margaret I had never seen.) A sudden serene gravity would show that she had seen one, and she would get into the four-foot punt that was used as a ferry and

bring it over very slowly, with rather
stiff movements of her long arms, to
exactly the right place. When she had
got the punt up on the gravel her serious
brow would relax and she would smile
at one and shake hands and say something
friendly, like, "Father thought you'd be
over this afternoon, it being so fine, so
he's saved some ducks' eggs for tea."
And then one took the pole from her and
brought her back to the island, though
probably one did not mount the steps
to the lawn for quite a long time. It
was so good to sit in the punt by the
landing-stage while Margaret dabbled her
hands in the black waters and forgot her
shyness as one talked. "She's such good
company. She's got an accurate mind
that would have made her a good en-
gineer, but when she picks up facts she
kind of gives them a motherly hug. She's
charity and love itself." (Again, I did
not say that I had seen her.) If people
drifted in to tea one had to talk to her

while she cut the bread and butter and the sandwiches in the kitchen, but in this year of floods few visitors cared to try the hard rowing below Bray Lock. So usually one sat down there in the boat, talking with a sense of leisure, as though one had all the rest of one's life in which to carry on this conversation, and noting how the reflected ripple of the water made a bright vibrant mark upon her throat and other effects of the scene upon her beauty; until the afternoon grew drowsy and she said, "Father will be wanting his tea." And they would go up and find old Allington, in white ducks, standing in the fringe of long grasses and cow-parsley on the other edge of the island, looking to his poultry or his rabbits. He was a little man with a tuft of copper-coloured hair rising from the middle of his forehead like a clown's curl, who shook hands hard and explained very soon that he was a rough diamond. Then they all had tea under the walnut tree where the canary's cage was hanging, and the ducks' eggs would be brought out, and Mr. Allington would talk much Thameside gossip: how the lock-keeper at Teddington had had his back broken by a swan, mad as swans are in May, and how they would lose their licence at the Dove-tail Arms if they were not careful, and how the man who kept the inn by Surly Hall was like to die, because after he had been cursing his daughter for two days for having run away with a soldier from Windsor Barracks, he had suddenly seen her white face in a clump of rushes in the river just under the hole in the garden fence. Margaret would sit quiet, round-eyed at the world's ways, and shy because of Chris.

So they would sit on that bright lawn until the day was dyed with evening blue, and Mr. Allington was more and more often obliged to leap into the punt to chase his ducks, who had started on a trip to Bray Lock, or to crawl into the undergrowth after rabbits similarly de-moralized by the dusk. And then Chris would say he had to go, and they would stand in a communing silence while the hearty voice of Mr. Allington shouted from midstream or under the alder-boughs a disregarded invitation to stay and have a bit of supper. In the liquefaction of colours which happens on a summer even-ing, when the green grass seemed like a precious fluid poured out on the earth and dripping over to the river, and the chestnut candles were no longer proud flowers, but just wet white lights in the humid mass of the tree, when the brown earth seemed just a little denser than the water, Margaret also participated. Chris explained this part of his story stumblingly, but I too have watched people I loved in the dusk and I know what he meant. As she sat in the punt while he ferried himself across it was no longer visible that her fair hair curled diffidently and that its rather wandering parting was

a little on one side; that her straight
brows, which were a little darker than
her hair, were nearly always contracted
in a frown of conscientious speculation;
that her mouth and chin were noble yet
delicate as flowers; that her shoulders
were slightly hunched because her young
body, like a lily stem, found it difficult
to manage its own tallness. She was then
just a girl in white who lifted a white
face or drooped a dull gold head. And
as that she was nearer to him than at
any other time. That he loved her, in
this twilight which obscured all the physical
details which he adored, seemed to him a
guarantee that theirs was a changeless love
which would persist if she were old or
maimed or disfigured. He stood beside the
crazy post where the bell hung and watched
the white figure take the punt over the black
waters, mount the grey steps and assume
their greyness, become a green shade in the
green darkness of the foliage-darkened
lawn, and he exulted in that guarantee.

How long this went on he had forgotten; but it continued for some time before there came the end of his life, the last day he could remember. I was barred out of that day. His lips told me of its physical appearances, while from his wet, bright eyes and his flushed skin, his beautiful signs of a noble excitement, I tried to derive the real story. It seemed that the day when he bicycled over to Monkey Island, happy because Uncle Ambrose had gone up to town and he could stay to supper with the Allingtons, was the most glorious day the year had yet brought. The whole world seemed melting into light. Cumulus clouds floated very high, like lumps of white light against a deep, glowing sky, and dropped dazzling reflections on the beaming Thames. The trees moved not like timber shocked by wind, but floatingly, like weeds at the bottom of a well of sunshine. When Margaret came out of the porch and paused, as she always did, to crush and smell the walnut leaf and shade her eyes with her hand, her white dress shone like silver.

She brought the punt across and said very primly, "Dad will be disappointed, he's gone up to town on business," and answered gravely, "That is very kind of you," when he took the punt-pole from her and said laughingly, "Never mind. I'll come and see you all the same." (I could see them as Chris spoke, so young and pale and solemn, with the intense light spilling all around them.) That afternoon they did not sit in the punt by the landing-stage, but wandered about the island and played with the rabbits and looked at the ducks, and were inordinately silent. For a long time they stood in the fringe of rough grass on the other side of the island and Margaret breathed contentedly that the Thames was so beautiful. Past the spit of sand at the far end of the island, where a great swan swanked to the empty reach that it would protect its mate against all comers, the river opened to a silver breadth between flat meadows stretching back to far rows of pin-thick black poplars, until it wound away to Windsor behind a line of high trees whose heads were bronze with un-opened buds and whose flanks were hidden by a hedge of copper-beech and crimson and white hawthorn. Chris said he would take her down to Dorney Lock in the skiff, and she got in very silently and obediently, but as soon as they were out in midstream she developed a sense of duty and said she could not leave the inn with just that boy. And then she went into the kitchen and, sucking in her lower lip for shyness, very conscien-tiously cut piles of bread and butter in case some visitors came to tea. Just when Chris was convincing her of the impossibility of any visitors arriving they came; a fat woman in a luscious pink blouse and an old chap who had been rowing in a tweed waistcoat. Chris went out, though Margaret laughed and trembled and begged him not to, and waited on them. It should have been a great lark but suddenly he hated them, and when they offered him a tip for pushing the boat off he snarled absurdly and ran back, miraculously relieved, to the bar-parlour.

Still Margaret would not leave the island. "Supposing," she said, "that Mr. Learoyd comes for his Bass." But she consented to walk with him to the wild part of the island, where poplars and alders and willows grew round a clearing in which white willow herb and purple figwort and here and there a potato flower, last ailing consequence of one of Mr. Allington's least successful enterprises, fought down to the fringe of iris on the river's lip. In this gentle jungle was a rustic seat, relic of a reckless aspiration on the part of Mr. Allington to make this a pleasure garden, and on it they sat until a pale moon appeared above the green cornfield on the other side of the river. "Not six yet," he said, taking out his watch. "Not six yet," she repeated. Words between them seemed to bear a significance apart from their meaning. Then a heron flapped gigantic in front of the moon and swung in wide circles round the willow tree before them. "Oh, look!" she cried. He seized the hand she flung upwards and gathered her into his arms. They were so for long while the great bird's wings beat above them.

Afterwards she pulled at his hand. She wanted to go back across the lawn and walk round the inn, which looked mournful as unlit houses do by dusk. They passed beside the green and white stucco barrier of the veranda and stood on the three-cornered lawn that shelved high over the stream at the island's end, regarding the river, which was now something more wonderful than water, because it had taken to its bosom the rose and amber glories of the sunset smouldering behind the elms and Bray church-tower. Birds sat on the telegraph wires that span the river there as the black notes sit on a stave of music. Then she went to the window of the parlour and rested her cheek against the glass, looking in. The little room was sad with twilight, and there was nothing to be seen but Margaret's sewing-machine on the table and the enlarged photograph of Margaret's mother over the mantelpiece, and the views of Tintern Abbey framed in red plush, and on the floor, the marigold pattern making itself felt through the dusk, Mr. Allington's carpet slippers. "Think of me sitting in there," she whispered, "not knowing you loved me." Then they went into the bar and drank milk, while she walked about fingering familiar things with an absurd expression of exaltation, as though that day she was fond of everything, even the handles of the beer engine.

When there had descended on them a night as brilliant as the day, he drew her out into the darkness, which was sweet with the scent of walnut leaves, and they went across the lawn, bending beneath the chestnut boughs, not to the wild part of the island, but to a circle of smooth turf divided from it by a railing of wrought iron. On this stood a small Greek temple, looking very lovely in the moonlight. He had never brought Margaret here before because Mr. Allington had once told him, spatulate forefinger at his nose, that it had been built by the Dook for his excesses, and it was in the quality of his love for her that he could not bear to think of her in connection with anything base. But to-night there was nothing anywhere but beauty. He lifted her in his arms and carried her within the columns and made her stand in a niche above the altar. A strong stream of moonlight rushed upon her there; by its light he could not tell if her hair was white as silver or yellow as gold, and again he was filled with exultation because he knew that it would not have mattered if it had been white. His love was changeless. Lifting her down from the niche, he told her so. And as he spoke her warm body melted to nothingness in his arms. The columns that had stood so hard and black against the quivering tide of moonlight and starlight tottered and dissolved. He was lying in a hateful world where barbed-wire entanglements showed impish knots against a livid sky full of booming noise and splashes of fire and wails for water, and the stretcher bearers were hurting his back intolerably.

Chris fell to blowing out the candles, and I, perhaps because the egotistical part of me was looking for something to say that would make him feel me devoted and intimate, could not speak.

Suddenly he desisted, stared at a candle flame, and said: "If you had seen the way she rested her cheek against the glass and looked into the little room, you'd understand that I can't say, 'Yes, Kitty's my wife, and Margaret somehow just nothing at all.'"

"Of course you can't," I murmured.

We gripped hands, and he brought down on our conversation the finality of darkness.

IV

NEXT morning it appeared that the
chauffeur had to take the Rolls-Royce up
to town to get a part replaced, and
Margaret could not be brought from
Wealdstone till the afternoon. It fell to
me to fetch her. "At least," Kitty had
said, "I might be spared that." Before
I started I went to the pond on the hill's
edge. It is a place where autumn lives
half the year, for even when the spring
lights tongues of green fire in the undergrowth and the valley shows sunlit between the tree trunks, here the pond is
fringed with yellow bracken and tinged
bramble, and the water flows amber over
last winter's leaves. Through this brown
gloom, darkened now by a surly sky,
Chris was taking the skiff, standing in the
stern and using his oar like a gondolier.

88

He had come down here soon after breakfast, driven from the house by the strangeness of all but the outer walls, and discontented with the ground because everywhere but this wet intractable spot bore the marks of Kitty's genius. After lunch there had been another attempt to settle down, but, with a grim glare at a knot of late Christmas roses bright in a copse that fifteen years ago had been dark, he went back to the russet-eaved boat-house and this play with the skiff. It was a boy's sport, and it was dreadful to see him turn a middle-aged face as he brought the boat inshore.

"I'm just going down to fetch Margaret," I said.

He thanked me for it.

"But, Chris, I must tell you. I've seen Margaret. She came up here, so kind and gentle, to tell us you were wounded. She's the greatest dear in the world. But she's not as you think of her. She's old, Chris. She isn't beautiful any more. She's

89

drearily married. She's seamed and scored and ravaged by squalid circumstances. You can't love her when you see her."

"Didn't I tell you last night," he said, "that that doesn't matter?" He dipped his oar to a stroke that sent him far away from me. "Bring her soon. I shall wait for her down here."

Wealdstone is not, in its way, a bad place; it lies in the lap of open country and at the end of every street rise the green hill of Harrow and the spires of Harrow School. But all the streets are long and red and freely articulated with railway arches, and factories spoil the sky-line with red angular chimneys, and in front of the shops stand little women with backs ridged by cheap stays, who tapped their upper lips with their forefingers and made other feeble, doubtful gestures as though they wanted to buy something and knew that if they did they would have to starve some other appetite. When we asked them the way they turned to us faces sour with thrift. It was a town of people who could not do as they liked. And here Margaret lived, in a long road of red brick boxes, flecked here and there with the pink blur of almond blossom, which debouched on a flat field where green grass rose up rank through clay mould blackened by coal dust from the railway line and the adjacent goods yard. Mariposa, which was the last house in the road, did not even have an almond tree. In her front garden, which seemed to be imperfectly reclaimed from the greasy field, yellow crocus and some sodden squills just winked, and the back, where a man was handling a spade without mastery, presented the austere appearance of an allotment. And not only did Margaret live in this place; she belonged to it. When she opened the door she gazed at me with watering eyes and in perplexity stroked her disordered hair with a floury hand. Her face was sallow with heat, and beads of perspiration glittered in the deep dragging line between her nostrils and the corners of her mouth.

She said, "He's home?"

I nodded.

She pulled me inside and slammed the door. "Is he well?"

"Quite," I answered.

Her tense stare relaxed. She rubbed her hands on her overall and said, "You'll excuse me. It's the girl's day out. If you'll step into the parlour. . . ."

So in her parlour I sat and told her how it was with Chris and how greatly he desired to see her. And as I spoke of his longing I turned my eyes away from her, because she was sitting on a sofa, upholstered in velveteen of a sickish green, which was so low that her knees stuck up in front of her and she had to clasp them with her seamed floury hands; and I could see that the skin of her face was damp. And then my voice failed me as I looked round the room, because I saw just what Margaret had seen that evening

92

fifteen years ago when she had laid her cheek to the parlour window at Monkey Island. There was the enlarged photograph of Margaret's mother over the mantelpiece; on the walls were the view of Tintern Abbey, framed in red plush; between the rickety legs of the china cupboard was the sewing-machine; and tucked into the corner between my chair and the fender were a pair of carpet slippers. All her life long Margaret, who in her time had partaken of the inalienable dignity of a requited love, had lived with men who wore carpet slippers in the house. I turned my eyes away again and this time looked down the garden at the figure that was not so much digging as exhibiting his incapacity to deal with a spade. He was sneezing very frequently, and his sneezes made the unbuckled straps at the back of his waistcoat wag violently. I supposed him to be Mr. William Grey.

I had finished the statement of our sad

case; and I saw that though she had not moved, clasping her knees in a set hideous attitude, the tears were rolling down her cheeks. "Oh, don't! Oh, don't!" I exclaimed, standing up. Her tear-stained immobility touched the heart. "He's not so bad—he'll get quite well. . . ."

"I know, I know," she said miserably. "I don't believe that anything bad would be allowed to happen to Chris for long. And I'm sure," she said kindly, "you're looking after him beautifully. But when a thing you had thought had ended fifteen years ago starts all over again, and you're very tired. . . ." She drew one of those dreadful hands across her tears, her damp skin, her rough, bagging overall. "I'm hot. I've been baking. You can't get a girl nowadays that understands the baking." Her gaze became remote and tender, she said in a manner that was at once argumentative and narrative, as though she were telling the whole story to a neighbour over the garden wall, "I

94

suppose I ought to say that he isn't right
in his head and I'm married—but oh!"
she cried, and I felt as though after much
fumbling with damp matches and many
doubts as to whether there was any oil
in the wick I had lit the lamp at last,
"I want to see him so! It's wrong—I
know it's wrong, but I am so glad Chris
wants to see me too!"

"You'll do him good!" I found myself raising my voice to the pitch she had
suddenly attained as though to keep her
at it. "Come now!"

She dipped suddenly to compassion.
"But the young lady?" she asked timidly.
"She was upset last time I went. I've
often wondered if I did right in going.
Even if Chris has forgotten her," she
gave out with an air of exposition, "he'll
want to do what's right. He couldn't
bear to hurt her."

"That's true," I said. "You do know
our Chris. He watches her out of the
corner of his eye, even when he's feeling

at his worst, to see she isn't wincing. But she sent me here to-day."

"*Oh!*" cried Margaret, glowing. "She must have a lovely nature!"

I lost suddenly the thread of the conversation. I could not talk about Kitty. She appeared to me at that moment a faceless figure with flounces, just as most of the servants at Baldry Court appear to me as faceless figures with caps and aprons. There were only two real people in the world, Chris and this woman whose personality was sounding through her squalor like a beautiful voice singing in a darkened room, and I was absorbed in a mental vision of them. You know how the saints and the prophets are depicted in the steel engravings in old Bibles; so they were standing, in flowing white robes, on rocks against a pitch black sky, a strong light beating on their eyes upturned in ecstasy, and their hands outstretched to receive the spiritual blessing of which the fierce rays were an emanation. Into that rapt silence I desired to break, and I whispered irrelevantly, "Oh, nothing, nothing is too good for Chris," while I said to myself, "If she were really like that, solemn and beatified," and my eyes returned to look despairingly on her ugliness. But she was really like that. She had responded to my irrelevant murmur of adoration by just such a solemn and beatified appearance as I had imagined. Her grave eyes were up-turned, those terrible hands lay palm upwards on her knees as though to receive the love of which her radiance was an emanation. And then, at a sound in the kitchen, she snatched my exaltation from me by suddenly turning dull. "I think that's Mr. Grey come in from his gardening. You'll excuse me. . . ."

Through the open door I heard a voice saying in a way which suggested that its production involved much agitation of a prominent Adam's apple. "Well, dear, seeing you had a friend I thought I'd better slip up and change my gardening trousers." I do not know what she said to him, but her voice was soft and comforting and occasionally girlish and interrupted by laughter, and I perceived from its sound that with characteristic gravity she had accepted it as her mission to keep loveliness and excitement alive in his life. "An old friend of mine has been wounded," was the only phrase I heard, but when she drew him out into the garden under the window she had evidently explained the situation away, for he listened docilely as she said, "I've made some rock-cakes for your tea. And if I'm late for supper there's a dish of macaroni cheese you must put in the oven and a tin of tomatoes to eat with it. And there's a little rhubarb and shape." She told them off on her fingers, and then whisked him round and buckled the wagging straps at the back of his waistcoat. He was a lank man with curly grey hairs growing from every place where it is inadvisable that hairs should grow, from the inside of his ears, from his nostrils, on the back of his hands; but he looked pleased when she touched him and said in a devoted way, "Very well, dear. Don't worry about me. I'll trot along after tea and have a game of draughts with Mr. Podds." She answered, "Yes, dear. And now get on with those cabbages. You're going to keep me in lovely cabbages just as you did last year, won't you, darling?" She linked arms with him and took him back to his digging.

When she came back into the parlour again she was wearing that yellowish raincoat, that hat whose hearse plumes nodded over its sticky straw, that grey alpaca skirt. I first defensively clutched my hands. It would have been such agony to the finger tips to touch any part of her apparel. And then I thought of Chris, to whom a second before I had hoped to bring a serene comforter. I perceived clearly that that ecstatic woman lifting her eyes and her hands to the benediction of love was Margaret as she existed in eternity; but this was Margaret as she existed in time, as the fifteen years between Monkey Island and this damp day in Ladysmith Road had irreparably made her. Well, I had promised to bring her to him.

She said, "I'm ready," and against that simple view of her condition I had no argument. But when she paused by the painted drain pipe in the hall and peered under contracted brows for that unveracious tortoise-shell handle, I said hastily, "Oh, don't trouble about an umbrella."

"I'll maybe need it walking home," she pondered.

"But the car will bring you back."

"Oh, that will be lovely!" She laughed nervously, looking very plain. "Do you know, I know the way we're coming together is terrible, but I can't think of a meeting with Chris as anything but a kind of treat. I've got a sort of party feeling now!"

As she held the gate open for me she looked back at the house. "It is a horrid little house, isn't it?" she asked. She evidently desired sanction for a long suppressed discontent.

"It isn't very nice," I agreed.

"They put cows sometimes into the field at the back," she went on, as if conscientiously counting her blessings. "I like that. But otherwise it isn't much."

"But it's got a very pretty name," I said, laying my hand on the raised metal letters that spelt "Mariposa" across the gate.

"Ah, isn't it!" she exclaimed, with the smile of the inveterate romanticist. "It's Spanish, you know, for butterfly."

Once we were in the automobile she became a little sullen with shyness because she felt herself so big and clumsy, her clothes so coarse against the fine up-holstery, the silver vase of Christmas roses, and all the deliberate delicacy of Kitty's car. She was afraid of the chauffeur, as the poor are always afraid of menservants, and ducked her head when he got out to start the car. To recall her to ease and beauty I told her that though Chris had told me all about their meeting he knew nothing of their parting, and that I wished very much to hear what had happened. And in a deep, embarrassed voice she began to tell me about Monkey Island. It was strange that both Chris and she spoke of it as though it were not a place, but a magic state which largely explained the actions performed in it. Strange too that both of them should describe meticulously the one white hawthorn that stood among the poplars by the ferryside; I suppose that a thing that one has looked at with somebody one loves acquires for ever after a special significance. She said that her father had gone there when she was fourteen. After Mrs. Allington had been taken away by a swift and painful death the cheer of his Windsor hostelry had

102

become intolerable to the man. He regarded the whole world as her grave; and the tipsy sergeants in scarlet and the carter crying for a pint of four-half, and the horses dipping their mild noses to the trough in the courtyard, all seemed to be defiling it by their happy, silly appetites. So they went to Monkey Island, whose utter difference was a healing, and settled down happily in its green silence. All the summer was lovely; quiet kind people, schoolmasters who fished, men who wrote books, married couples who still loved solitude, used to come and stay in the bright little inn. And all the winter was lovely too; her temperament could see an adventure in taking up the carpets because the Thames was coming into the coffee-room. That was the tale of her life for four years. With her head on one side, and an air of judging this question by the light of experience, she pronounced that she had then been happy.

Then, one April afternoon, Chris landed

at the island, and by the first clean quick movement of tying up his boat made her his slave. I could imagine that it would be so. He was so wonderful when he was young; he possessed in great measure the loveliness of young men, which is like the loveliness of the spry foal or the sapling, but in him it was vexed into a serious and moving beauty by the inhabiting soul. When the sunlight lay on him, discerning the gold hairs on his brown head, or when he was subject to any other physical pleasure there was always reserve in his response to it; from his eyes, which though grey were somehow dark with speculation, one perceived that he was distracted by participation in some spiritual drama. To see him was to desire intimacy with him so that one might intervene between this body which was formed for happiness and this soul which cherished so deep a faith in tragedy. . . . Well, she gave Chris ducks' eggs for tea. "No one ever had ducks' eggs like father did. It was his way of feeding them. It didn't pay, of course, but they *were* good." Before the afternoon was out he had snared them all with the silken net of his fine manners; he had talked to father about his poultry and walked about the runs, and then as on many succeeding days he had laid his charm at the girl's feet. "But I thought he must be someone royal, and when he kept on coming I thought it must be for the ducks' eggs." Then her damp, dull skin flushed suddenly to a warm glory, and she began to stammer.

"I know all about that," I said quickly. I was more afraid that I should feel envy or any base passion in the presence of this woman than I have ever been of anything in my life. "I want to hear how you came to part."

"Oh," she cried. "It was the silliest quarrel. We had known how we felt for just a week. Such a week. Lovely weather we had, and father had noticed nothing. I didn't want him to, because

I thought father might want the marriage soon and think any delay a slight on me, and I knew we would have to wait. Eh, I can remember saying to myself, 'Perhaps five years,' trying to make it as bad as I could so that if we could marry sooner it would be a lovely surprise." She repeated it with soft irony. "Perhaps five years!"

"Well, then, on Thursday afternoon I'd gone on the backwater with Bert Wells, nephew to Mr. Wells who keeps the inn at Surly Hall. I was laughing out loud because he did row so funny. He's a town chap, and he was handling those oars for all the world as though they were teaspoons. The old dinghy just sat on the water like a hen on its chicks and didn't move, and he so sure of himself! I just sat and laughed and laughed. Then all of a sudden—*clang-clang!* the bell at the ferry. And there was Chris, standing up there under the poplars, his brows straight and black and not a smile on him. I felt very bad. We

picked him up in the dinghy and took
him across, and still he didn't smile. He
and I got on the island and Bert, who saw
there was something wrong, said, 'Well,
I'll toddle off.' And there I was on the
lawn with Chris, and he angry and somehow miles away. I remember him saying,
'Here I am, coming to say good-bye
because I must go away to-night, and I
find you larking with that bounder,' and
I said, 'Oh, Chris! I've known Bert all
my life, through him coming to his·uncle
for the holidays, and we weren't larking.
It was only that he couldn't row.' And
he went on talking and then it struck me
he wasn't trusting me as he would trust
a girl of his own class, and I told him so,
and he went on being cruel. Oh, don't
make me remember the things we said
to each other! It doesn't help. . . . At
last I said something awful and he said,
'Very well, I agree. I'll go,' and he
walked over to where the boy was chopping
wood and got him to take him over in the

punt. As he passed me he turned away his face. Well, that's all."

I had got the key at last. There had been a spring at Baldry Court fifteen years ago which was desolate for all that there was beautiful weather. Chris had lingered with Uncle Ambrose in his Thameside rectory as he had never lingered before, and old Mr. Baldry was filling the house with a sense of hot, apoplectic misery. All day he was up in town at the office and without explanation he had discontinued his noontide habit of ringing up his wife. All night he used to sit in the library looking over his papers and ledgers; the housemaids often found him in the morning asleep across his desk, very red, yet looking dead. The men he brought home to dinner treated him with a kindness and consideration which was not the tribute that that victorious and trumpeting personality was accustomed to exact; in the course of conversation with them he dropped braggartly cheerful hints of impending ruin, which it would have been humiliating to address to us directly. At last there came one morning when he said to Mrs. Baldry across the breakfast table, "I've sent for Chris. If the boy's worth his salt . . ." It was an appalling admission, like the groan of an old ship as her timbers shiver, from a man who doubted the capacity of his son as fathers always doubt the capacity of the children of their old age. It was that evening, as I went down to see the new baby at the lodge, that I met Chris coming up the drive. Through the blue twilight his white face had a drowned look. I remember it well because my surprise that he passed me without seeing me had made me perceive for the first time that he had never seen me at all save in the most cursory fashion; on the eye of his mind, I realized thenceforward, I had hardly impinged. That night he talked till late with his father and in the morning he had started for Mexico, to keep the mines going through the revolution, to keep the firm's head above water and Baldry Court sleek and hospitable, to keep everything bright and splendid save only his youth, which after that was dulled by care.

Something of this I told Margaret, to which she answered, "Oh, I know all that," and she went on with her story. On Sunday, three days after their quarrel, Mr. Allington was found dead in his bed. "I wanted Chris so badly, but he never came, he never wrote," and she fell into a lethargic disposition to sit all day and watch the Thames flow by, from which she was hardly roused by finding that her father had left her nothing save an income of twenty pounds a year in unrealizable stock. She negotiated the transfer of the lease of the inn to a publican and, after exacting a promise from the new hostess that she would forward all letters that might come, embarked upon an increasingly unfortunate career as a mother's help. First she fell into the hands of a noble Irish family in reduced circumstances named Murphy, whose conduct in running away and leaving her in a Brighton hotel with her wages and her board unpaid, still distressed and perplexed her. "Why did they do it?" she asked. "I liked them so. The baby was a darling and Mrs. Murphy had such a nice way of speaking. But it almost makes one think evil of people when they do a thing like that." After two years of less sensational but still uneasy adventures, she had come upon a large and needy family called Watson who lived at Chiswick, and almost immediately Mr. William Grey, who was Mrs. Watson's brother, had begun a courtship that sounded to me as though it had consisted of an incessant whining up at her protective instinct. "Mr. Grey," she said softly, as though stating his chief claim to affection, "has never been very successful." And still no letter ever came.

So, five years after she left Monkey Island, she married Mr. William Grey. Soon after their marriage he lost his job and was for some time out of work; later he developed a weak chest that needed constant attention. "But it all helped to pass the time," she said cheerfully and without irony. So it happened that it was not for many years that she had the chance of revisiting Monkey Island. At first there was no money and later there was the necessity of seeking the healthful breezes of Brighton or Bognor or Southend, which were the places in which Mr. Grey's chest oddly elected to thrive. And when those obstacles were removed she was lethargic; and also she had heard that the inn was not being managed as it ought to be, and she could not have borne to see the green home of her youth defiled. But then there had come a time when she had been very much upset; she glared a little wildly at me as she said this, as if she would faint if I asked her any questions. And then she had suddenly become obsessed with a desire to see Monkey Island once more.

"Well, when we got to the ferry Mr. Grey says, 'But mercy, Margaret, there's water all round it!' and I said, 'But, William, that's just it!'" They found that the island was clean and decorous again, for it had but recently changed hands. "Father and daughter the new people are, just like me and dad, and Mr. Taylor's something of dad's cut, too, but he comes from the North. But Miss Taylor's much handsomer than I ever was; a really big woman she is, and such lovely golden hair. They were very kind when they heard who I was; gave us duck and green peas for lunch and I did think of dad. They were nothing like as good as his ducks, but then I expect they paid. And then Miss Taylor took William out to look at the garden. I could see he didn't like it, for he's always shy with a showy woman, and I was going after them when Mr. Taylor said, 'Here, stop a minute, I've got something here that may interest you. Just come in here,' and he led me to the roller desk in the office. Out of a drawer he took twelve letters addressed to me in Chris's handwriting.

"He was a kind man. He put me into a chair and called Miss Taylor in and told her to keep William out in the garden as long as possible. At last I said, 'But Mrs. Hitchcock did say she'd send my letters on.' And he said, 'But Mrs. Hitchcock hadn't been three weeks before she bolted with a bookie from Bray. And after that Hitchcock mixed his drinks and got careless.' The Taylors had found these stuffed into the desk when they came."

"And what was in them?"

"For a long time I did not read them. I thought it was against my duty as a wife. But when I got that telegram saying he was wounded I went upstairs and read those letters. Oh, those letters. . . ."

She bowed her head and wept.

As the car swung through the gates of Baldry Court she sat up and dried her eyes. She looked out at the strip of turf, so bright that one would think it wet, and lit here and there with snowdrops and scillas and crocuses, that runs between the drive and the tangle of silver birch and bramble and fern. There is no æsthetic reason for that border; the common outside looks lovelier where it fringes the road with dark gorse and rough amber grasses. Its use is purely philosophic; it proclaims that here we estimate only controlled beauty, that the wild will not have its way within our gates, that it must be made delicate and decorated into felicity. Surely she must see that this was no place for beauty that has been not mellowed but lacerated by time, that no one accustomed to live here could help wincing at such external dinginess as hers. . . . But instead she said, "It's a big place. How poor Chris must have worked to keep it up." The pity of this woman was like a flaming sword. No one had ever before pitied Chris for the magnificence of Baldry Court. It had been our pretence that by wearing costly clothes and organizing a costly life we had been the servants of his desire. But she revealed the truth that although he did indeed desire a magnificent house, it was a house not built with hands.

But that she was wise, that the angels would of a certainty be on her side, did not make her any the less physically offensive to our atmosphere. All my doubts as to the wisdom of my expedition revived in the little time we had to spend in the hall waiting for the tea which I had ordered in the hope that it might help Margaret to compose her distressed face. She hovered with her back to the oak table, fumbling with her thread gloves, winking her tear-red eyes, tapping with her foot on the carpet, throwing her weight from one leg to the other, and constantly contrasted her appearance with

116

the new acquisition of Kitty's decorative
genius which stood so close behind her on
the table that I was afraid it might be
upset by one of her spasmodic movements. This was a shallow black bowl
in the centre of which crouched on hands
and knees a white naked nymph, her small
head intently drooped to the white flowers
that floated on the black waters all around
her. Beside the pure black of the bowl
her rusty plumes looked horrible; beside
that white nymph, eternally innocent of
all but the contemplation of beauty, her
opaque skin and her suffering were offensive; beside its air of being the coolly
conceived and leisurely executed production of a hand and brain lifted by their
rare quality to the service of the not
absolutely necessary, her appearance of
having but for the moment ceased to cope
with a vexed and needy environment
struck one as a cancerous blot on the
fair world. Perhaps it was absurd to
pay attention to this indictment of a

woman by a potter's toy, but that toy
happened to be also a little image of
Chris's conception of women. Exquisite
we were according to our equipment;
unflushed by appetite or passion, even
noble passion; our small heads bent intently on the white flowers of luxury
floating on the black waters of life; and
he had known none other than us. With
such a mental habit a man could not help
but wince at Margaret. I drank my tea
very slowly because I previsioned what
must happen in the next five minutes.
Down there by the pond he would turn
at the sound of those heavy boots on the
path, and with one glance he would assess
the age of her, the rubbed surface of her,
the torn fine texture, and he would show
to her squalid mask just such a blank face
as he had shown to Kitty the night
before. Although I have a gift for self-
pity I knew her case would then be worse
than mine; for it would be worse to see,
as she would see, the ardour in his eyes

give place to kindliness than never to have seen ardour there. He would hesitate, she would make one of her harried gestures and trail away with that wet patient look which was her special line. He would go back to his boyish sport with the skiff; I hoped the brown waters would not seem too kind. She would go back to Mariposa, sit on her bed, and read those letters. . . .

"And now," she said brightly, as I put down my cup, "may I see Chris?" She had not a doubt of the enterprise.

I took her into the drawing-room and opened one of the French windows. "Go past the cedars to the pond," I told her. "He is rowing there."

"That is nice," she said. "He always looks so lovely in a boat."

I called after her, trying to hint the possibility of a panic breakdown to their meeting, "You'll find he's altered. . . ."

She cried gleefully, "Oh, I shall know him."

119

As I went upstairs I became conscious that I was near to a bodily collapse; I suppose that the truth is that I was physically so jealous of Margaret that it was making me ill. But suddenly, just like a tired person dropping a weight they know is precious but that they cannot carry for another moment, my mind refused to consider the situation any longer and turned to the perception of material things. I leant over the banisters and looked down at the fineness of the hall: the deliberate figure of the nymph in her circle of black water, the clear pink and white of Kitty's chintz, the limpid surface of the oak, the gay reflected colours in the panelled walls. I said to myself, "If everything else goes there is always this to fall back on," and I went on, pleased that I was wearing delicate stuffs and that I had a smooth skin, pleased that the walls of the corridor were so soft a twilight blue, pleased that through a far-off open door came a stream of light that made the carpet blaze its stronger blue. And when I saw that it was the nursery door that was open, and that in Nanny's big chair at the window Kitty sat, I did not care about the peaked face she lifted, its fairness palely gilt by the March sunlight, nor the tremendous implications of the fact that she had come to the dead child's nursery though she had not washed her hair. I said sternly, because she had forgotten that we lived in the impregnable fortress of a gracious life, "Oh, Kitty, that poor battered thing outside."

She stared so grimly out into the garden that my eyes followed her stare.

It was one of those draggled days, so common at the end of March, when a garden looks at its worst. The wind that was rolling up to check a show of sunshine had taken away the cedar's dignity of solid shade, had set the black firs beating their arms together and had filled the sky with glaring grey clouds that dimmed the brilliance of the crocus. It was to give gardens a point on days such as these, when the planned climax of this flower bed and that stately tree goes for nothing, that the old gardeners raised statues in their lawns and walks, large things with a subject, mossy Tritons or nymphs with an urn, that held the eye. Even so in this unrestful garden one's eye lay on the figure in the yellow raincoat that was standing still in the middle of the lawn.

How her near presence had been known by Chris I do not understand, but there he was, running across the lawn as night after night I had seen him in my dreams running across No Man's Land. I knew that so he would close his eyes as he ran; I knew that so he would pitch on his knees when he reached safety. I assumed that at Margaret's feet lay safety, even before I saw her arms brace him under the armpits with a gesture that was not passionate, but rather the movement of one carrying a wounded man from under fire. But even when she had raised his head to the level of her lips, the central issue was not decided. I covered my eyes and said aloud, "In a minute he will see her face, her hands." But although it was a long time before I looked again they were still clinging breast to breast. It was as though her embrace fed him, he looked so strong as he broke away. They stood with clasped hands, looking at one another (they looked straight, they looked delightedly!), and then, as if resuming a conversation tiresomely interrupted by some social obligation, drew together again and passed under the tossing branches of the cedar to the wood beyond. I reflected, while Kitty wept, how entirely right Chris had been in his assertion that to lovers innumerable things do not matter.

V

AFTER the automobile had taken Margaret away Chris came to us as we sat in the drawing-room and, after standing for a while in the glow of the fire, hesitantly said, "I want to tell you that I know it is all right. Margaret has explained to me."

Kitty crumpled her sewing into a white ball. "You mean, I suppose, that you know I'm your wife. I'm pleased that you describe that as knowing 'it's all right,' and grateful that you have accepted it at last—on Margaret's authority. This is an occasion that would make any wife proud." Her irony was as faintly acrid as a caraway seed, and never afterwards did she reach even that low pitch of violence, for from that mild forward droop of the head with which he received the mental lunge she realized suddenly that this was no pretence and that something as impassable as death lay between them. Thereafter his proceedings evoked no comment but suffering. There was nothing to say when all day, save for those hours of the afternoon which Margaret spent with him, he sat like a blind man waiting for his darkness to lift. There was nothing to say when he did not seem to see our flowers, yet kept till they rotted on the stalk the daffodils which Margaret brought from the garden that looked like an allotment. So Kitty lay about like a broken doll, face downward on a sofa with one limp arm dangling to the floor, or protruding stiff feet in fantastic slippers from the end of her curtained bed; and I tried to make my permanent wear that mood which had mitigated the end of my journey with Margaret, a mood of intense perception in which my strained mind settled on every vivid object that came under my eyes and tried to identify myself with its brightness and its lack of human passion. This does not mean that I passed my day in a state of joyous appreciation; it means that many times in the lanes of Harrowweald I have stood for long looking up at the fine tracery of bare boughs against the hard, high spring sky while the cold wind rushed through my skirts and chilled me to the bone, because I was afraid that when I moved my body and my attention I might begin to think. Indeed grief is not the clear melancholy the young believe it. It is like a siege in a tropical city. The skin dries and the throat parches as though one were living in the heat of the desert; water and wine taste warm in the mouth and food is of the substance of the sand; one snarls at one's company; thoughts prick one through sleep like mosquitoes. . . . .

A week after my journey to Wealdstone I went to Kitty to ask her to come for a walk with me and found her stretched on her pillows, holding a review of her under-clothing. She refused bitterly and added, "Be back early. Remember Dr. Gilbert Anderson is coming at half-past four, He's our last hope. And tell that woman she must see him. He says he wants to see everybody concerned," and continued to look wanly at the frail luminous silks her maid brought her, as a speculator who had cornered the article for which there had been no demand might look at his damnably numerous, damnably unprofitable freights. So I went out alone into a soft day, with the dispelled winter lurking above in high dark clouds under which there ran quick fresh currents of air, and broken shafts of insistent sunshine that spread a grey clarity of light in which every colour showed sharp and strong. On the breast that Harrowweald turns to the south they had set a lambing-yard, whose pale lavender hurdles and gold strewn straw and orange drinking-trough were new gay notes on the opaque winter green of the slope, and the apprehensive bleatings of the ewes wound about the hill like a river of sound as they were driven up a lane hidden by the hedge. The lines of bare elms darkening the plains below made it seem as though the tide of winter had fallen and left this promontory bare and sparkling in the spring. I liked it so much that I opened the gate and went and sat down on a tree that had been torn up by the roots in the great gale last year, but had not yet resigned itself to death and was bravely decking itself with purple elm-flowers. That pleased me too, and I wished I had some-one with me to enjoy this artless little show of the new year. I had not really wanted Kitty; the companions I needed were Chris and Margaret. Chris would have talked as he loved to do when he looked at leisure on a broad valley, about ideas which he had to exclude from his ordinary hours lest they should break the power of business over his mind, and Margaret would have gravely watched

128

the argument from the shadow of her broad hat to see that it kept true, like a housewife watching a saucepan of milk lest it should boil over. They were naturally my friends, these gentle speculative people. Then suddenly I was stunned with jealousy. It was not their love for one another that caused me such agony at that moment; it was the thought of the things their eyes had rested upon together. I imagined that white hawthorn among the poplars by the ferry on which they had looked fifteen years ago at Monkey Island, and it was more than I could bear. I thought how even now they might be exclaiming at the green smoke of the first buds on the brown undergrowth round the pond, and at that I slid off the tree-trunk and began walking very quickly down the hill. The red cows drank from the pond cupped by the willow roots, a raw-boned stallion danced clumsily because warmth was running through the ground, I found a stream in the fields and

followed it till it became a shining dyke
embanked with glowing green and gold
mosses in the midst of woods; and the
sight of those things was no sort of joy,
because my vision was solitary. I wanted
to end my desperation by leaping from a
height, and I climbed on a knoll and flung
myself face downwards on the dead leaves
below.

I was now utterly cut off from Chris.
Before, when I looked at him I knew an
instant ease in the sight of the short
golden down on his cheeks, the ridge of
bronze flesh above his thick fair eye-
brows. But now I was too busy reassur-
ing him by showing a steady, undistorted
profile crowned by a neat proud sweep of
hair instead of the tear-darkened mask
he always feared, ever to have enough
vitality left over to enjoy his presence. I
spoke in a calm voice full from the chest
quite unfluted with agony; I read *Country
Life* with ponderous interest; I kept my
hands, which I desired to wring, in doeskin

gloves for most of the day; I played with
the dogs a great deal and wore my thickest
tweeds; I pretended that the slight heaviness of my features is a correct indication
of my temperament. The only occasion
when I could safely let the sense of him
saturate me as it used was when I met
Margaret in the hall as she came or went.
She was very different now; she had a
little smile in her eyes as though she were
listening to a familiar air played far away,
her awkwardness seemed indecision as to
whether she should walk or dance to that
distant music, her shabbiness was no
more repulsive than the untidiness of a
child who had been so eager to get to the
party that it has not let its nurse fasten
its frock. Always she extended a hand
in an unbuttoned black thread glove and
said, "It's another fine day again," or
diffidently, as Kitty continued to withhold
her presence, "I hope Mrs. Baldry is
keeping well." Then as our hands touched
he was with us, invoked by our common

adoration; I felt his rough male texture and saw the clear warmth of his brown and gold colouring. I thought of him with the passion of exile. To Margaret it was a call, and she moved past me to the garden, holding her hands in front of her as though she bore invisible gifts, and pausing on the step of the French window to smile to herself, as if in her heart she turned over the precious thought, "He is here. This garden holds him." My moment, my small sole subsistence, ended in a feeling of jealousy as ugly and un-mental as sickness. This was the saddest spring.

Nothing could mitigate the harshness of our rejection. You may think we were attaching an altogether fictitious import-ance to what was merely the delusion of a madman. But every minute of the day, particularly at those trying times when he strolled about the house and grounds with the doctors, smiling courteously, but without joy, and answering their questions

with the crisp politeness of a man shaking
off an inquisitive commercial traveller in
a hotel smoking-room, it became plain
that if madness means liability to wild
error about the world, Chris was not mad.
It was our peculiar shame that he had
rejected us when he had attained to something saner than sanity. His very loss of
memory was a triumph over the limita-
tions of language which prevent the mass
of men from making explicit statements
about their spiritual relationships. If he
had said to Kitty and me, "I do not
know you," we would have gaped; if he
had expanded his meaning and said,
"You are nothing to me; my heart is
separate from your hearts," we would
have wept at an unkindness he had not
intended. But by the blankness of those
eyes which saw me only as a disregarded
playmate and Kitty not at all save as a
stranger who had somehow become a
decorative presence in his home and the
orderer of his meals he let us know com-

pletely where we were. Even though I lay weeping at it on the dead leaves I was sensible of the bitter rapture that attends the discovery of any truth. I felt, indeed, a cold intellectual pride in his refusal to remember his prosperous maturity and his determined dwelling in the time of his first love, for it showed him so much saner than the rest of us, who take life as it comes, loaded with the inessential and the irritating. I was even willing to admit that this choice of what was to him reality out of all the appearances so copiously presented by the world, this adroit recovery of the dropped pearl of beauty, was the act of genius I had always expected from him. But that did not make less agonizing this exclusion from his life.

I could not think clearly about it. I suppose that the subject of our tragedy, written in spiritual terms, was that in Kitty he had turned from the type of woman that makes the body conqueror of the soul and in me from the type that mediates between the soul and the body and makes them run even and unhasty like a well-matched pair of carriage horses, and had given himself to a woman whose bleak habit it was to champion the soul against the body. But I saw it just as a fantastic act of cruelty that I could only think of as a conjunction of calamitous images. I think of it happening somewhere behind the front, at the end of a straight road that runs by a line of ragged poplars between mud flats made steel-bright with floods pitted by the soft slow rain. There, past a church that lacks its tower, stand a score of houses, each hideous with patches of bare bricks that show like sores through the ripped-off plaster and uncovered rafters which stick out like broken bones. There are people still living here. A slut sits at the door of a filthy cottage, counting some dirty linen and waving her bare arms at some passing soldiers. And at another

135

house there is a general store with strings
of orange onions and bunches of herbs
hanging from the roof, a brown gloom
rich with garlic and humming with the
flies that live all the year round in French
village shops, a black cat rubbing her
sleekness against the lintel. It is in there
that Chris is standing, facing across the
counter an old man in a blue blouse, with
a scar running white into the grey thickets
of his beard, an old man with a smile
at once lewd and benevolent, repulsive
with dirt and yet magnificent by reason of
the Olympian structure of his body. I
think he is the soul of the universe,
equally cognisant and disregardful of every
living thing, to whom I am no more dear
than the bare-armed slut at the neigh-
bouring door. And Chris is leaning on the
counter, his eyes glazed. (This is his
spirit; his body lies out there in the drizzle
at the other end of the road.) He is
looking down on two crystal balls that the
old man's foul strong hands have rolled

across to him. In one he sees Margaret; not in her raincoat and her nodding plumes but as she is transfigured in the light of eternity. Long he looks there; then drops a glance to the other, just long enough to see that in its depths Kitty and I walk in bright dresses through our glowing gardens. We had suffered no transfiguration, for we are as we are and there is nothing more to us. The whole truth about us lies in our material seeming. He sighs a deep sigh of delight and puts out his hand to the ball where Margaret shines. His sleeve catches the other one and sends it down to crash in a thousand pieces on the floor. The old man's smile continues to be lewd and benevolent, he is still not more interested in me than in the bare-armed slut; and Chris is wholly enclosed in his intentness on his chosen crystal. No one weeps for this shattering of our world. . . .

I stirred on the dead leaves as though I had really heard the breaking of the globe and cried out, "Gilbert Anderson, Gilbert Anderson must cure him." Heaven knows that I had no reason for faith in any doctor, for during the past week so many of them, sleek as seals with their neatly brushed hair and their frock-coats, had stood round Chris and looked at him with the consequenceless delibera-tion of a plumber. Their most successful enterprise had been his futile hypnotism. He had submitted to it as a good-natured man submits to being blindfolded at a children's party and under its influence had recovered his memory and his middle-aged personality, had talked of Kitty with the humorous tenderness of the English husband and had looked posses-sively about him. But as his mind came out of the control he exposed their lie that they were dealing with a mere break-down of the normal process by pushing away this knowledge and turning to them the blank wall, all the blanker because it was unconscious, of his resolution not to

know. I had accepted that it would
always be so. But at that moment I had
so great a need to throw off my mood of
despair, so insupportably loaded with all
the fantastic images to which my fevered
mind transmuted the facts of our tragedy,
that I filled myself with a gasping, urgent
faith in this new doctor. I jumped up
and pushed through the brambles to the
hedge that divided the preserves in which
I was trespassing from our own woods,
breathless because I had let it go past four
and I had still to find Chris and Margaret
for the doctor's visit at the half-hour.

There had been a hardening of the light
during the afternoon that made the dear
familiar woods rich and sinister and, to the
eye, tropical. The jewel-bright buds on
the soot-black boughs, and the blue valley
distances, smudged here and there with
the pink enamel of villa roofs and seen
between the black and white intricacies of
the birch-trunks and the luminous grey
pillars of the beeches, hurt my wet eyes as

might beauty blazing under an equatorial sun. There was a tropical sense of danger too, for I walked as apprehensively as though a snake coiled under every leaf, because I feared to come on them when he was speaking to her without looking at her, or thinking in silence while he played with her hand. Embraces do not matter; they merely indicate the will to love and may as well be followed by defeat as victory. But disregard means that now there needs to be no straining of the eyes, no stretching forth of the hands, no pressing of the lips, because theirs is such a union that they are no longer conscious of the division of their flesh. I know it must be so; a lonely life gives one opportunities of thinking these things out. I could not have borne to see signs of how he had achieved this intimacy with the woman whom a sudden widening of the downward vista showed as she leant her bent back, ridged by those cheap stays, against a birch that some special

140

skill of the forester had made wonderful for its straight slenderness. Against the clear colours of the bright bare wood her yellow raincoat made a muddy patch, and as a dead bough dropped near her she made a squalid dodging movement like a hen. She was not so much a person as an implication of dreary poverty, like an open door in a mean house that lets out the smell of cooking cabbage and the screams of children. Doubtlessly he sat somewhere close to her, lumpishly content. I thought distractedly how necessary it was that Gilbert Anderson should cure him, and tried to shout to her but found my throat full of sobs. So I broke my way down through the fern and bramble and stood level with them, though still divided by some yards of broken ground.

It was not utter dullness not to have anticipated the beauty that I saw. No one could have told. . . . They had taken the mackintosh rug out of the dinghy and spread it on this little space of clear grass,

I think so that they could look at a scattering of early primroses in a pool of white anemones at an oak-tree's foot. She had run her dreadful hands over the rug so that it lay quite smooth and comfortable under him when at last he felt drowsy and turned on his side to sleep. He lay there in the confiding relaxation of a sleeping child, his hands unclenched and his head thrown back so that the bare throat showed defencelessly. Now he was asleep and his face undarkened by thought one saw how very fair he really was. And she, her mournfully vigilant face pinkened by the cold river of air sent by the advancing evening through the screen of rusted gold bracken was sitting beside him, just watching.

I have often seen people grouped like that on the common outside our gates, on Bank Holidays. Most often the man has a handkerchief over his face to shade him from the sun and the woman squats beside him and peers through the undergrowth to see that the children come to no harm as they play. It has sometimes seemed to me that there was a significance about it. You know when one goes into the damp odorous coolness of a church in a catholic country and sees the kneeling worshippers, their bodies bent stiffly and reluctantly and yet with abandonment as though to represent the inevitable bending of the will to a purpose outside the individual, or when under any sky one sees a mother with her child in her arms, something turns in one's heart like a sword and one says to oneself, "If humanity forgets these attitudes there is an end to the world." But people like me, who are not artists, are never sure about people they don't know. So it was not until now, when it happened to my friends, when it was my dear Chris and my dear Margaret who sat thus englobed in peace as in a crystal sphere, that I knew that it was the most significant as it was the loveliest attitude in the world. It means that the woman has gathered the soul of the man into her soul and is keeping it warm in love and peace so that his body can rest quiet for a little time. That is a great thing for a woman to do. I know there are things at least as great for those women whose independent spirits can ride fearlessly and with interest outside the home park of their personal relationships, but independence is not the occupation of most of us. What we desire is greatness such as this which had given sleep to the beloved. I had known that he was having bad nights at Baldry Court, in that new room with the jade-green painted walls and the lapis lazuli fire-place, which he had found with surprise to be his instead of the remembered little room with the fishing-rods. But I had not been able to do anything about it.

It was not fair that by the exercise of a generosity which seemed as fortuitous a possession as a beautiful voice a woman should be able to do such wonderful

things for a man. For sleep was the least
of her gifts to him. What she had done
in leading him into this quiet magic circle
out of our life, out of the splendid house
which was not so much a house as a vast
piece of space partitioned off from the
universe and decorated partly for beauty
and partly to make our privacy more
insolent, out of the garden where the
flowers took thought as to how they should
grow and the wood made formal as a
pillared aisle by forestry, may be judged
from my anguish in being left there alone.
Indeed she had been generous to us all,
for at her touch our lives had at last fallen
into a pattern; she was the sober thread
whose interweaving with our scattered
magnificences had somehow achieved the
design that otherwise would not appear.
Perhaps even her dinginess was part of
her generosity, for in order to fit into
the pattern one sometimes has to forgo
something of one's individual beauty.
That is why women like us do not wear
145

such obviously lovely dresses as cocottes, but clothe themselves in garments that by their slight neglect of the possibilities of beauty declare that there are such things as thrift and restraint and care for the future. And so I could believe of Margaret that her determined dwelling in places where there was not enough of anything, her continued exposure of herself to the grime of squalid living, was unconsciously deliberate. The deep internal thing that had guided Chris to forgetfulness had guided her to poverty so that when the time came for her meeting with her lover there should be not one intimation of the beauty of suave flesh to distract him from the message of her soul. I looked upward at this supreme act of sacrifice and glowed at her private gift to me. My sleep, though short, was now dreamless. No more did I see his body rotting into union with that brown texture of corruption which is No Man's Land, no more did I see him slipping softly down the parapet

146

into the trench, no more did I hear voices talking in a void: "*Help me, old man, I've got no legs.* . . ."—"*I can't, old man, I've got no hands.* . . ." They could not take him back to the Army as he was. Only that morning as I went through the library he had raised an appalled face from the pages of a history of the war. "Jenny, it can't be true—that they did *that*—to Belgium? Those funny, quiet, stingy people. . . ." And his soldierly knowledge was as deeply buried as this memory of that awful August. While her spell endured they could not send him back into the hell of war. This wonderful kind woman held his body as safely as she held his soul.

I was so grateful that I was forced to go and sit down on the rug beside her. It was an intrusion, but I wanted to be near her. She did not look surprised when she turned to me her puckered brows, but smiled through the ugly fringe of vagrant hairs the weather had plucked from under the hard rim of her hat. It was part of her loveliness that even if she did not understand an act she could accept it.

Presently she leant over to me across his body and whispered, "He's not cold. I put the overcoat on him as soon as he was fairly off. I've just felt his hands and they're as warm as toast." If I had whispered like that I would have wakened him.

Soon he stirred, groped for her hand and lay with his cheek against its rough palm. He was awake by then but liked to lie so.

In a little she shook her hand away and said, "Get up and run along to the house and have some hot tea. You'll catch your death lying out here."

He caught her hand again. It was evident that for some reason the moment was charged with ecstasy for them both.

It seemed as though there were a softer air in this small clearing than anywhere else in the world. I stood up with my

148

back against a birch and said negligently, knowing now that nothing could really threaten them, "There is a doctor coming at half-past four who wants to see you both." It cast no shadow on their serenity. He smiled upward, still lying on his back, and hailed me, "Hallo, Jenny." But she made him get up and help her fold the rug. "It's not right to keep a doctor waiting in these times," she declared, "so overworked they are, poor men, since the war. . . ." As I led the way up through the woods to the house I heard her prove her point by an illustrative anecdote about something that had happened down her road. I heard, too, their footsteps come to a halt for a space. I think her grey eyes had looked at him so sweetly that he had been constrained to take her in his arms.

VI

I FELT—I remember it with the little perk of self-approbation with which one remembers any sort of accurate premonition even if its fulfilment meant disaster —a cold hand close round my heart as we turned the corner of the house and came on Dr. Gilbert Anderson. I was startled, to begin with, by his unmedical appearance. He was a little man with winking blue eyes, a flushed and crumpled forehead, a little grey moustache that gave him the profile of an amiable cat, and a lively taste in spotted ties, and he lacked that appetiteless look which is affected by distinguished practitioners. He was at once more comical and more suggestive of power than any other doctor I had ever seen, and this difference was emphaszied by his unexpected occupation. A tennis ball which he had discovered somewhere had roused his sporting instincts, and he was trying at what range it was possible to kick it between two large stones which he had placed close together in front of the steps up to the house. It was his chubby absorption in this amusement which accounted for his first gape of embarrassment. "Nobody about in there—we professional men get so little fresh air——" he said bluffly, and blew his nose in a very large handkerchief, from whose folds he emerged with perfect self-possession. "You," he said to Chris, with a naïve adoption of the detective tone, "are the patient." He rolled his blue eye on me, took a good look, and as he realized I did not matter shook off the unnecessary impression like a dog coming out of water. He faced Margaret as though she were the nurse in charge of the case and gave her a brisk little nod. "You're Mrs. Grey. I shall want to talk to you later. Mean-

time—this man. I'll come back." He
indicated by a windmill gesture that we
should go into the house and swung off
with Chris.

She obeyed; that sort of woman always
does what the doctor orders. But I
delayed for a moment to stare after this
singular specialist, to side-track my foreboding by pronouncing him a bounder,
to wish, as my foreboding persisted, that
like a servant I could give notice because
there was "always something happening
in the house." Then, as the obedient
figure at the top of the stairs was plainly
shivering under its shoddy clothes in the
rising wind that was polishing the end of
the afternoon to brightness, I hastened
to lead her into the hall. We stood about
uneasily in its gloaming. As usual the
shining old panelling seemed aware of all
that was going on and conscious that it
was older and better than the people who
owned it; the white nymph drooped over
the black waters of the bowl and reminded

one how nice, how neat and nice, life used to be; the chintz sang the vulgar old English country-house song. Margaret looked round her and said, in a voice slightly flattened by the despondency which she evidently shared with me, "It is nice to have everything ready that people can want, and everything in its place. I used to do it at Monkey Island Inn. It was not grand like this, of course, but our visitors always came back a second time." Abstractedly and yet with joy she fingered the fine work of the table leg.

There was a noise above us like the fluttering of doves. Kitty was coming downstairs in a white serge dress against which her hands were rosy; a woman with such lovely little hands never needed to wear flowers. By her kind of physical discipline she had reduced her grief to no more than a slight darkening under the eyes, and for this moment she was glowing. I knew it was because she was going to meet a new man and anticipated the kindling of admiration in his eyes, and I smiled, contrasting her probable prefiguring of Dr. Anderson with the amiable rotundity we had just encountered. Not that it would have made any difference if she had seen him. Beautiful women of her type lose, in this matter of admiration alone, their otherwise tremendous sense of class distinction; they are obscurely aware that it is their civilizing mission to flash the jewel of their beauty before all men, so that they shall desire it and work to get the wealth to buy it, and thus be seduced by a present appetite to a tilling of the earth that serves the future. There is, you know, really room for all of us; we each have our peculiar use.

"The doctor's talking to Chris outside," I said.

"Ah," breathed Kitty. I found, though the occasion was a little grim, some entertainment in the two women's faces, so mutually intent, so differently fair, the one a polished surface that reflected light, like a mirror hung opposite a window, the other a lamp grimed by the smoke of careless use but still giving out radiance from its burning oil. Margaret was smiling wonderingly up at this prettiness; but Kitty seemed to be doing some brainwork.

"How do you do, Mrs. Grey?" she said suddenly, shaking out her cordiality as one shakes out a fan. "It's very kind of you to come. Won't you go upstairs and take off your things?"

"No, thank you," answered Margaret shyly, "I shall have to go away so soon."

"Ah, do!" begged Kitty prettily.

It was, of course, that she did not want Margaret to meet the specialist in those awful clothes, but I did not darken the situation by explaining that this disaster had already happened. Instead I turned to Margaret an expression which conveyed that this was an act of hospitality the refusal of which we would find wounding, and to that she yielded as I knew she would. She followed me upstairs and along the corridors very slowly, like a child paddling in a summer sea; she enjoyed the feeling of the thick carpet underfoot, she looked lingeringly at the pictures on the wall, occasionally she put a finger to touch a vase as if by that she made its preciousness more her own. Her spirit, I could see, was as deeply concerned about Chris as was mine, but she had such faith in life that she retained serenity enough to enjoy what beauty she came across during her period of waiting. Even her enjoyment was indirectly generous; when she came into my room the backward flinging of her head and her deep "Oh!" recalled to me what I had long forgotten, how fine were its proportions, how clever the grooved arch above the window, how like the evening sky my blue curtains. . . .

"And the lovely things you have on

your dressing-table," she commented.
"You must have very good taste." The
charity, that changed my riches to a
merit! As I helped her to take off her
raincoat, and reflected that Kitty would
not be pleased when she saw that the
removal of the garment disclosed a purple
blouse of stuff called moirette that servants use for petticoats, she exclaimed
softly Kitty's praises. "I know I
shouldn't make personal remarks, but
Mrs. Baldry is lovely. She has three
circles round her neck. I've only two."
It was a touching betrayal that she possessed that intimate knowledge of her
own person which comes to women who
have been loved. I could not for the
life of me have told you how many circles
there were round my neck. Plainly discontented with herself in the midst of all
this fineness she said diffidently, "Please,
I would like to do my hair," so I pulled
the arm-chair up to the dressing-table and
leant on its back while she, sitting shyly

on its very edge, unpinned her two long braids, so thick, so dull.

"You've lovely hair," I said.

"I used to have nice hair," she mourned, "but these last few years I've let myself go." She made half-hearted attempts to smooth the straggling tendrils on her temples, but presently laid down her brush and clicked her tongue against her teeth. "Tchk! I hope that man's not worrying Chris. "

There was no reassurance ready, so I went to the other side of the room to put her hat down on a chair, and stayed for a moment to pat its plumes and wonder if nothing could be done with it. But it was, as surgeons say, an inoperable case. So I just gloomed at it and wished I had not let this doctor interpose his plumpness between Chris and Margaret, who since that afternoon seemed to me as not only a woman whom it was good to love, but as a patron saint must appear to a catholic, as an intercessory being whose kindliness could be daunted only by some special and incredibly malicious decision of the Supreme Force. I was standing with eyes closed and my hands abstractedly stroking the hat which was the emblem of her martyrdom, and I was thinking of her in a way that was a prayer to her, when I heard her sharp cry   That she should cry out sharply, whose essence was a patient silence . .   I turned very quickly.

She was standing up, and in her hand she held the photograph of Oliver that stands on my dressing-table. It is his last photograph, the one taken just a week before he died.

"Who is this?"

"The only child Chris ever had. He died five years ago."

"Five years ago?"

Why did it matter so?

"Yes."

"He died five years ago, my Dick." Her eyes grew great. "How old was he?"

159

"Just two."

"My Dick was two. . . ." We both were breathing hard. "Why did he die?"

"We never knew. He was the loveliest boy, but delicate from his birth. At the end he just faded away, with the merest cold."

"So did my Dick. A chill. We thought he would be up and about the next day, and he just——"

Her awful gesture of regret was suddenly paralysed. She seemed to be fighting her way to a discovery.

"It's—it's as if," she stammered, "they each had half a life. . . ."

I felt the usual instinct to treat her as though she were ill, because it was evident that she was sustained by a mystic interpretation of life. But she had already taught me something, so I stood aside while she fell on her knees, and wondered why she did not look at the child's photograph, but pressed it to her bosom as though to staunch a wound. I thought, as I have often thought before, that the childless have the greatest joy in children, for to us they are just slips of immaturity lovelier than the flowers and with a power over the heart, but to mothers they are fleshy cables binding one down to such profundities of feeling as the awful agony that now possessed her. For although I knew I would have accepted it with rapture, because it was the result of intimacy with Chris, its awfulness appalled me. Not only did it make my body hurt with sympathy, it shook the ground beneath my feet. For that her serenity, which a moment before had seemed as steady as the earth and as all-enveloping as the sky, should be so utterly dispelled made me aware that I had of late been underestimating the cruelty of the order of things. Lovers are frustrated; children are not begotten that should have had the loveliest life, the pale usurpers of their birth die young.

Such a world will not suffer magic circles to endure.

The parlourmaid knocked at the door. "Mrs. Baldry and Dr. Anderson are waiting in the drawing-room, ma'am."

Margaret reassumed her majesty, and put her white face close to the glass as she pinned up her braids. "I knew there was a something," she moaned, and set the hairpins all awry. She said nothing more; but the slow gesture with which, as we were about to leave the room, she laid her hand across the child's photograph, somehow convinced me that we were not to be victorious.

When we went into the drawing-room we found Dr. Anderson, plump and expository, balancing himself on the balls of his feet on the hearthrug and enjoying the caress of the fire on his calves, while Kitty, showing against the dark frame of her oak chair like a white rosebud that was still too innocent to bloom, listened with that slight reservation of

162

the attention customary in beautiful women.

"A complete case of amnesia," he was saying, as Margaret, white-lipped yet less shy than I had ever seen her, went to a seat by the window and I sank down on the sofa. "His unconscious self is refusing to let him resume his relations with his normal life, and so we get this loss of memory."

"I've always said," declared Kitty, with an air of good sense, "that if he would make an effort. . . ."

"Effort!" He jerked his round head about. "The mental life that can be controlled by effort isn't the mental life that matters. You've been stuffed up when you were young with talk about a thing called self-control—a sort of barmaid of the soul that says, 'Time's up, gentlemen,' and 'Here, you've had enough.' There's no such thing. There's a deep self in one, the essential self, that has its wishes. And if those wishes are suppressed by the superficial self—the self

163

that makes, as you say, efforts and usually makes them with the sole idea of putting up a good show before the neighbours— it takes its revenge. Into the house of conduct erected by the superficial self it sends an obsession. Which doesn't, owing to a twist that the superficial self, which isn't candid, gives it, seem to bear any relation to the suppressed wish. A man who really wants to leave his wife develops a hatred for pickled cabbage which may find vent in performances that lead straight to the asylum. But that's all technical!" he finished bluffly. "My business to understand it, not yours. The point is, Mr. Baldry's obsession is that he can't remember the latter years of his life. Well——" his winking blue eyes drew us all into a community we hardly felt— "what's the suppressed wish of which it's the manifestation?"

"He wished for nothing," said Kitty. "He was fond of us, and he had a lot of money."

"Ah, but he did!" countered the doctor gleefully. He seemed to be enjoying it all. "Quite obviously he has forgotten his life here because he is discontented with it. What clearer proof could you need than the fact you were just telling me when these ladies came in—that the reason the War Office didn't wire to you when he was wounded was that he had forgotten to register his address? Don't you see what that means?"

"Forgetfulness," shrugged Kitty, "he isn't business-like." She had always nourished a doubt as to whether Chris was really, as she put it, practical; his income and his international reputation weighed as nothing against his so evident inability to pick up pieces at sales.

"One forgets only those things that one wants to forget. It's our business to find out why he wanted to forget this life."

"He can remember quite well when he

165

is hypnotized," she said obstructively. She had quite ceased to glow

"Oh, hypnotism's a silly trick. It releases the memory of a dissociated personality which can't be related—not possibly in such an obstinate case as this —to the waking personality. I'll do it by talking to him. Getting him to tell his dreams." He beamed at the prospect. "But you—it would be such a help if you could give me any clue to this discontent."

"I tell you," said Kitty, "he was not discontented till he went mad."

He caught at last the glint of her rising temper. "Ah," he said, "madness is an indictment not of the people one lives with, only of the high gods! If there was anything it's evident that it was not your fault——" A smile sugared it, and knowing that where he had to flatter his dissecting hand had not an easy task he turned to me, whose general appearance suggests that flattery is not part of my

166

daily diet. "You, Miss Baldry, you've known him longest. . . ."

"Nothing and everything was wrong," I said at last. "I've always felt it. . . ." A sharp movement of Kitty's body confirmed my deep, old suspicion that she hated me.

He went back further than I thought he would. "His relations with his father and mother, now?"

"His father was old when he was born, and always was a little jealous of him. His mother was not his sort. She wanted stupid son, who would have been satisfied with shooting."

He laid down a remark very softly, like a hunter setting a snare.

"He turned, then, to sex with a peculiar need."

It was Margaret who spoke, shuffling her feet under her chair.

"Yes, he was always very dependent." We gaped at her, who said this of our splendid Chris, and I saw that she was

not as she had been. There was a direct-
ness of speech, a straight stare, that was
for her a frenzy. "Doctor," she said, her
mild voice roughened, "what's the use
of talking? You can't cure him." She
caught her lower lip with her teeth and
fought back from the brink of tears.
"Make him happy, I mean. All you can
do is to make him ordinary."

"I grant you that's all I do," he said.
It queerly seemed as though he was
experiencing the relief one feels on
meeting an intellectual equal. "It's my
profession to bring people from various
outlying districts of the mind to the
normal. There seems to be a general
feeling it's the place where they ought
to be. Sometimes I don't see the urgency
myself."

She continued without joy. "I know
how you could bring him back. A memory
so strong that it would recall everything
else—in spite of his discontent."

The little man had lost in a moment

his glib assurance, his knowingness about the pathways of the soul. "Well, I'm willing to learn."

"Remind him of the boy," said Margaret.

The doctor ceased suddenly to balance on the balls of his feet. "What boy?"

"They had a boy."

He looked at Kitty. "You told me nothing of this!"

"I didn't think it mattered," she answered, and shivered and looked cold as she always did at the memory of her unique contact with death. "He died five years ago."

He dropped his head back, stared at the cornice, and said with the soft malignity of a clever person dealing with the slow-witted, "These subtle discontents are often the most difficult to deal with." Sharply he turned to Margaret. "How would you remind him?"

"Take him something the boy wore, some toy they used to play with."

Their eyes met wisely. "It would have to be you that did it."

Her face assented.

Kitty said, "I don't understand. Why does it matter so much?" She repeated it twice before she broke the silence that Margaret's wisdom had brought down on us. Then Dr. Anderson, rattling the keys in his trouser pockets and swelling red and perturbed, answered, "I don't know why. But it does."

Kitty's voice soared in satisfaction. "Oh! Then it's very simple. Mrs. Grey can do it now. Jenny, take Mrs. Grey up to the nursery. There are lots of things up there."

Margaret made no movement, but continued to sit with her heavy boots resting on the edge of their soles. Dr. Anderson searched Kitty's face, exclaimed "Oh, well!" and flung himself into an armchair so suddenly that the springs spoke.

Margaret smiled at that and turned to

me, "Yes, take me to the nursery, please."
Yet as I walked beside her up the stairs
I knew this compliance was not the indication of any melting of this new steely
sternness. The very breathing that I
heard as I knelt beside her at the nursery
door and fitted the key in the lock,
seemed to come from a different and a
harsher body than had been hers before.
I did not wonder that she was feeling
bleak, since in a few moments she was to
go out and say the words that would
end all her happiness, that would destroy
all the gifts her generosity had so difficultly amassed. Well, that is the kind of
thing one has to do in this life.

But hardly had the door opened and
disclosed the empty sunny spaces swimming with motes before her old sweetness
flowered again. She moved forward
slowly, tremulous and responsive and
pleased, as though the room's loveliness
was a gift to her; she stretched out her
hands to the clear sapphire walls and the

bright fresco of birds and animals with a
young delight. So, I thought, might a
bride go about the home her husband had
secretly prepared for her. Yet when she
reached the hearth and stood with her
hands behind her on the fireguard, looking about her at all the exquisite devices
of our nursery to rivet health and amusement on our reluctant little visitor, it
was so apparent that she was a mother
that I could not imagine how it was that
I had not always known it. It has sometimes happened that painters who have
kept close enough to earth to see a
heavenly vision have made pictures of
the Assumption of the Blessed Virgin,
which do indeed show women who could
bring God into the world by the passion
of their motherhood. "Let there be life,"
their suspended bodies seem to cry out
to the universe about them, and the very
clouds under their feet change to cheru-
bim. As Margaret stood there, her hands
pressed palm to palm beneath her chin,

and a blind smile on her face, she looked even so.

"Oh, the fine room!" she cried. "But where's his cot?"

"It isn't here. This is the day nursery The night nursery we didn't keep. It's just a bedroom now."

Her eyes shone at the thought of the cockered childhood this had been. "I couldn't afford to have two nurseries. It makes all the difference to the wee things." She hung above me for a little as I opened the ottoman and rummaged among Oliver's clothes. "Ah, the lovely little frocks! Did she make them? Ah, well, she'd hardly have the time, with this great house to see to. But I don't care much for baby frocks. The babies themselves are none the happier for them. It's all for show." She went over to the rocking-horse and gave a ghostly child a ride. For long she hummed a tuneless song into the sunshine and retreated far away into some maternal dream. "He was too young for this," she said. "His daddy must have given him it. I knew it. Men always give them presents above their age. They're in such a hurry for them to grow up. We like them to take their time, the loves. But where's his engine? Didn't he love puffer-trains? Of course, he never saw them. You're so far from the railway station. What a pity! He'd have loved them so. Dick was so happy when I stopped his pram on the railway bridge on my way back from the shops, and he could sit up and see the puffers going by." Her distress that Oliver had missed this humble pleasure darkened her for a minute. "Why did he die! You didn't overtax his brain? He wasn't taught his letters too soon?"

"Oh, no," I said. I couldn't find the clothes I wanted. "The only thing that taxed his little brain were the prayers his Scotch nurse taught him, and he didn't bother much over them. He would say

'Jesus, tender leopard,' instead of 'Jesus, tender shepherd,' as though he liked it better that way. . . ."

'Did you ever! The things they say! He'd a Scotch nurse. They say they're very good. I've read in the papers the Queen of Spain has one." She had gone back to the hearth again and was playing with the toys on the mantelpiece. It was odd that she showed no interest in my search for the most memorable garment; a vivacity which played above her tear-wet strength, like a ball of St. Jacob's fire on the mast of a stout ship, made me realize she still was strange. "The toys he had! His nurse didn't let him have them all at once. She held him up and said, 'Baby, you must choose!' and he said, 'Teddy—please—Nanny!' and wagged his head at every word."

I had laid my hand on them at last. I wished, in the strangest way, that I hadn't. Yet of course it had to be. "That's just what he did do."

175

As she felt the fine kid skin of the clockwork dog her face began to twitch. "I thought perhaps my baby had left me because I had so little to give him. But if a baby could leave all this——." She cried flatly, as though constant repetition in the night had made it as instinctive a reaction to suffering as a moan. "I want a child! I want a child!" Her arms invoked the life that had been squandered in this room. "It's all gone so wrong!" she fretted, and her voice dropped to a solemn whisper. "They each had only half a life. . . ."

I had to steady her. She could not go to Chris and shock him, not only by her news, but also by her agony. I rose and took her the things I had found in the ottoman and the toy cupboard. "I think these are the best things to take. This is one of the blue jerseys he used to wear. This is the red ball he and his father used to play with on the lawn."

Her hard hunger for the child that was not melted into a tenderness for the child that had been. She looked broodingly at what I carried, then laid a kind hand on my arm. "You've chosen the very things he will remember. Oh, you poor girl. . . ."

I found that from her I could accept even pity.

She nursed the jersey and the ball, changed them from arm to arm and held them to her face. "I think I know the kind of boy he was. A man from the first." She kissed them, folded up the jersey and neatly set the ball upon it on the ottoman, and regarded them with tears. "There, put them back. That's all I wanted them for. All I came up here for."

I stared.

"To get near Chris's boy," she moaned. "You thought I meant to take them out to Chris?" She wrung her hands, her weak voice quavered at the sternness of her resolution. "How can I?"

I grasped her hands. "Why should you bring him back?" I said.

I might have known there was deliverance in her yet.

Her slow mind gathered speed.

"Either I never should have come," she pleaded, "or you should let him be." She was arguing not with me, but with the whole hostile reasonable world. "Mind you, I wasn't sure if I ought to come the second time, seeing we both were married and that. I prayed and read the Bible, but I couldn't get any help. You don't notice how little there is in the Bible really till you go to it for help. But I've lived a hard life and I've always done my best for William, and I know nothing in the world matters so much as happiness. If anybody's happy you ought to let them be. So I came again. Let him be. If you knew how happy he was just pottering round the garden. Men do love a garden. He could just go on. It can go on so easily." (But there was a shade of doubt in her voice; she was pleading not only with me but with fate.) "You wouldn't let them take him away to the asylum. You wouldn't stop me coming. The other one might, but you'd see she didn't. Oh, do just let him be. . . .

"Put it like this." She made such explanatory gestures as I have seen cabmen make over their saucers of tea round a shelter. "If my boy had been a cripple—he wasn't; he had the loveliest limbs—and the doctors had said to me, 'We'll straighten your boy's legs for you, but he'll be in pain all the rest of his life,' I'd not have let them touch him. . . .

"I seemed to have to tell them that I knew a way. I suppose it would have been sly to sit there and not tell them. I told them anyhow. But oh! I can't do it. Go out and put an end to the poor love's happiness! After the time he's had, the war and all. And then he'll

179

have to go back there! I can't! I can't!"

I felt an ecstatic sense of ease. Everything was going to be right. Chris was to live in the interminable enjoyment of his youth and love. There was to be a finality about his happiness which usually belongs only to loss and calamity; he was to be as happy as a ring cast into the sea is lost, as a man whose coffin has lain for centuries beneath the sod is dead. Yet Margaret continued to say, and irritated me by the implication that the matter was not settled, "I oughtn't to do it, ought I?"

"Of course not! Of course not!" I cried heartily, but the attention died in her eyes. She stared over my shoulder at the open door, where Kitty stood.

The poise of her head had lost its pride, the shadows under her eyes were black like the marks of blows, and all her loveliness was diverted to the expression of grief. She held in her arms her Chinese

180

sleeve dog, a once prized pet that had
fallen from favour and now was only to
be met whining upward for a little love
at every passer in the corridors, and it
sprawled leaf-brown across her white frock,
wriggling for joy at the unaccustomed
embrace. That she should at last have
stooped to lift the lonely little dog was
a sign of her deep unhappiness. Why
she had come up I do not know, nor
why her face puckered with tears as she
looked in on us. It was not that she had
the slightest intimation of our decision,
for she could not have conceived that we
could follow any course but that which
was obviously to her advantage. It was
simply that she hated to see this strange
ugly woman moving about among her
things. She swallowed her tears and
passed on, to drift like her dog about
the corridors.

Now, why did Kitty, who was the
falsest thing on earth, who was in tune
with every kind of falsity, by merely

suffering somehow remind us of reality?
Why did her tears reveal to me what I
had learned long ago, but had forgotten
in my frenzied love, that there is a draught
that we must drink or not be fully human?
I knew that one must know the truth.
I knew quite well that when one is adult
one must raise to one's lips the wine of
the truth, heedless that it is not sweet
like milk but draws the mouth with its
strength, and celebrate communion with
reality, or else walk for ever queer and
small like a dwarf. Thirst for this sacra-
ment had made Chris strike away the
cup of lies about life that Kitty's white
hands held to him, and turn to Margaret
with this vast trustful gesture of his loss
of memory. And helped by me she had
forgotten that it is the first concern of
love to safeguard the dignity of the beloved, so that neither God in his skies
nor the boy peering through the hedge
should find in all time one possibility for
contempt, and had handed him the trivial

toy of happiness. We had been utterly negligent of his future, blasphemously careless of the divine essential of his soul. For if we left him in his magic circle there would come a time when his delusion turned to a senile idiocy; when his joy at the sight of Margaret disgusted the flesh, because his smiling mouth was slack with age; when one's eyes no longer followed him caressingly as he went down to look for the first primroses in the wood, but flitted here and there defensively to see that nobody was noticing the doddering old man. Gamekeepers would chat kindly with him and tap their foreheads as he passed through the copse, callers would be tactful and dangle bright talk before him. He who was as a flag flying from our tower would become a queer-shaped patch of eccentricity on the country-side, the stately music of his being would become a witless piping in the bushes. He would not be quite a man.

183

I did not know how I could pierce Margaret's simplicity with this last cruel subtlety, and turned to her stammering. But she said, "Give me the jersey and the ball."

The rebellion had gone from her eyes and they were again the seat of all gentle wisdom.

"The truth's the truth," she said, "and he must know it."

I looked up at her, gasping yet not truly amazed, for I had always known she could not leave her throne of righteousness for long, and she repeated, "The truth's the truth," smiling sadly at the strange order of this earth.

We kissed, not as women, but as lovers do; I think we each embraced that part of Chris the other had absorbed by her love. She took the jersey and the ball and clasped them as though they were a child. When she got to the door she stopped and leaned against the lintel. Her head fell back, her eyes closed, her mouth was contorted as though she swallowed bitter drink.

I lay face downwards on the ottoman and presently heard her poor boots go creaking down the corridors. Through the feeling of doom that filled the room as tangibly as a scent I stretched out to the thought of Chris. In the deep daze of devotion which followed recollection of the fair down on his cheek, the skin burnt brown to the rim of his grey eyes, the harsh and diffident masculinity of him, I found comfort in remembering that there was a physical gallantry about him which would still, even when the worst had happened, leap sometimes to the joy of life. Always, to the very end, when the sun shone on his face or his horse took his fences well, he would screw up his eyes and smile that little stiff-lipped smile. I nursed a feeble glow at that. "We must ride a lot," I planned. And then Kitty's heels tapped on the polished floor and her skirts swished as she sat down in the arm-chair, and I was distressed by the sense, more tiresome than a flickering light, of someone fretting.

She said, "I wish she would hurry up. She's got to do it sooner or later."

My spirit was asleep in horror. Out there Margaret was breaking his heart and hers, using words like a hammer, looking wise, doing it so well.

"Aren't they coming back?" asked Kitty. "I wish you'd look."

There was nothing in the garden. Only a column of birds swimming across the lake of green light that lay before the sunset.

A long time after Kitty spoke once more. "Jenny, do look again."

There had fallen a twilight which was a wistfulness of the earth. Under the cedar boughs I dimly saw a figure mothering something in her arms. Almost had she dissolved into the shadows; in another moment the night would have her. With his back turned on this fading happiness

Chris walked across the lawn. He was looking up under his brows at the over-arching house as though it were a hated place to which, against all his hopes, business had forced him to return. He stepped aside to avoid a patch of brightness cast by a lighted window on the grass; lights in our house were worse than darkness, affection worse than hate elsewhere. He wore a dreadful decent smile; I knew how his voice would resolutely lift in greeting us. He walked not loose limbed like a boy, as he had done that very afternoon, but with the soldier's hard tread upon the heel. It recalled to me that, bad as we were, we were yet not the worst circumstance of his return. When we had lifted the yoke of our embraces from his shoulders he would go back to that flooded trench in Flanders under that sky more full of flying death than clouds, to that No Man's Land where bullets fall like rain on the rotting faces of the dead. . . .

187

"Jenny, aren't they there?"

"They're both there."

"Is he coming back?"

"He's coming back."

"Jenny, Jenny! How does he look?"

"Oh. . . ." How could I say it? "Every inch a soldier."

She crept behind me to the window, peered over my shoulder and saw.

I heard her suck her breath with satisfaction. "He's cured!" she whispered slowly. "He's cured!"

REBECCA WEST

Cicily Isabel Fairfield was born in London. Her father had come from County Kerry, Ireland, and she acquired her early education in Edinburgh. She adopted her pen name, Rebecca West, from the strong-willed character of that name in Ibsen's social drama, *Rosmersholm*, in which she once acted in her late teens. She began to appear in print as a journalist and political writer in London as early as 1911, in *The Freewoman*, and was soon deeply involved in the causes of feminism and social reform. These interests were prominent in her journalism and later were echoed in her novels, her biographical writings, criticism, satire, travel and history, which have alternated and supplemented each other throughout her long career.

Her first book, *Henry James*, was published in 1916. Her eight novels include *The Return of the Soldier* (1918), *The Judge* (1922), *Harriet Hume: A London Fantasy* (1929)—all three published by Virago: *The Harsh Voice* (1935), *The Thinking Reed* (1936), *The Fountain Overflows* (1956) and *The Birds Fall Down* (1966). In 1977 a selection of her greatest work, *A Celebration*, was published which included a portion of her latest novel, as yet incomplete: *This Real Night*, a sequel to *The Fountain Overflows*.

Her only child, Anthony West (b. 1914), was the son of the novelist H. G. Wells. In 1930 she married Henry Maxwell Andrews, the banker, and began a lifelong companionship at their country house, Ibstone, in Buckinghamshire, with visits to London and many travels together, including the journey to Yugoslavia that inspired *Black Lamb and Grey Falcon*, her two-volume magnum opus. She was created a Dame Commander of the British Empire in 1959. After her husband's death in 1968 she returned to London where she now lives.